Through Blood by Fate

Through Blood by Fate

Dawning Hour Chronicles 

A. Rose Weir

Voyages Publishing: Aurora Prism Editions

Published by Voyages Publishing: Aurora Prism Editions
Dunedin, FL, 34698
Cover by Heathen South Artworks
Editor Evelyn Presley

Hardcover ISBN 978-1-964732-04-6
Paperback ISBN 978-1-964732-03-9
Ebook ISBN 978-1-964732-02-2

CONTENTS

CONTENTS

"What bothered her the most was that she couldn't decide if this had all happened because of the connection to Rosalina or if the events were already in motion before tonight. Her friends would say it's not one or the other. That every moment is a reaction to a million years of interactions reaching the present."

This quote from the book is a point of belief for me that I've woven into the fabric of this fictional world. Growing up, I tried to appeal to everyone, read them so well I could predict their decisions to avoid chaotic outcomes, only to realize the world is a complex tapestry full of decisions and reactions that impacted every moment in the past, present, and future. I experienced personal growth at a young age, but we all know this to be accurate at some age; sometimes, we misplaced our fears, sorrows, or anger at countless points throughout time.

Not only do our actions today leave a chain reaction to the future, but to think someone's actions even a hundred years ago could be a part of our current lives. Be it someone defying social standards of marriage, those times anyone has escaped abuse, or bringing a seemingly impossible child into the world. The power and impact of using caring words, a smile, and simple gestures can be an invisible force, never realized to its fullest, even as they weave and maintain connections years later. The mysteries of the universe are endless, and the ripples they left remain today.

At the core of this book are values of loyalty, found family, personal growth, justice, and a sense of responsibility. It wasn't until I found my chosen family and met my lovely wife that I transitioned from surviving day-to-day, planning on just making it to the end, to embracing life's potential. After some time, the closed-off parts of me opened up. Suddenly, I had so much more self-accepting to do until I finally felt free enough to work on dreams I had put aside. Dreams, once buried by negativity and heavy burdens, came to life after realizing I had barely scratched the surface of what life could offer.

Speaking to readers and fans from numerous backgrounds and experiences, I must admit, at times, it can be hard to believe that there is a reason for everything. Coming from a faith to a spiritual point in my own life, I often focus on the contributions I can make. I once heard an excellent analogy for religion and spirituality. It explained the difference between them using a fish in a bag of water versus one in the sea. The fish in the bag defines the boundaries of following rules and being told the difference between right and wrong, rather than being free to choose based on personal feelings and not desiring to hurt anyone.

I say if I didn't choose to follow the morals of someone I admired rather than the ones I was surrounded by, my life could be severely different. We all ponder the 'what-if' questions in our lives. What if I had met my wife earlier, what if I hadn't moved, and so on? This story dives headfirst into those doubts and limitless possibilities, acknowledging that eternity is a long time to exist without expecting someone or something to validate our choices.

As this is the series' first book, this begins where the characters find their paths in accepting personal growth amidst challenges that test the strong bonds formed in found family. Some conflicts have been in motion for years, while new threats take work and dedication to fulfill responsibilities in hopes of making amends for past faults. As you read, I encourage you to find the secrets buried in the details. Face what inner turmoil the story reveals. Immerse yourself in the characters' aspirations to exceed their perceived limits and be more than they thought possible.

The ideas that came to me when making Through Blood by Fate are the greatest gifts I have ever received. There were moments in my life that needed reflecting on to encourage the words that formed this piece as if it were the embodiment of my heart and soul. When reflections failed, I always had the people in my life and groups that I joined to learn from to thank for the support they all gave.

First, while it saddens me, I needed to take a moment to honor and thank Steven Weir in some way for having high hopes for me. For being the father I always needed. From difficulties facing certain emotions when writing characters to bringing the book to life after all the edits and reflections for this book has only been possible because my father-in-law wished I wouldn't give up before his passing. His reading interests may have been different than the direction I was motivated to begin my first novel, but I know he would celebrate this with me if he could.

Second, I thank Meaghan Weir (my wife) and Kristina (my sister) for seeing me through this journey. Long before them, I often asked myself where motivation and passion stemmed from. Why does love or pain bring about the drive we need in our lives? Because of them, I pushed through each personal battle I faced and made surprisingly significant strides in my work.

Last but not least, I thank the Tarpon Springs Writers and Authors Guild for being there to offer help anytime I was stuck. I can't know everything, but with them, I learned where to start and what to do next when I finish a book. They bring community to the members, celebrating the wins and helping those struggling to find what they need. It is always nice to have family and friends rallying for you, but a group that works like a team to reach your goals doesn't hurt.

Thank you all for making it possible to share this story with the readers, and thank you to all the readers for picking up this book.

Prologue

In Mid-November Hell's Kitchen, Jade, a newly arrived resident, took in the city's nightlife. Having finished unpacking that day, finding a place to grab a drink seemed a relatively good idea. The street has a few convenience stores, diners, and cafés. A bar sat just as one would expect. Music beats the doors to escape, loudly talking groups as they exit, overflowing with drunk men and women alike.

Before entering, an alluring fragrance of honeysuckle, coffee, and a hint of cedar is just up the road, calling to follow it. Despite being aware that the bar awaits, taking a few steps to find the source seems feasible until a sewage truck floods the scent away. The source of the fragrance was gone, yet the yearning for a drink surrounded by nightlife was still there.

Stepping into the bar, some patrons stopped chatting long enough to see if they recognized whoever was entering. No one knew the brunette-haired woman. Unfamiliar or not, that never stopped people from offering to buy her a drink. It took taking off her leather jacket, declining the first few men who greeted her, and sitting beside an attractive petite black-haired woman to send a noticeable message of lack of interest in anything but the fairer sex. Introducing herself as Jade, she supplied half-truths about just moving to the city, wanting to look around, only deciding to come in to step out of the cold for a few; she then captured the woman's story of why she was there.

Planning to stay for one drink turned into drinking until her turn would come up in karaoke, being someone who loved singing. The night felt young and endless when her fingers grasped the mic and lips parted to let the first vocal cords start the song. The crowd took a liking to her melody and began singing along loudly. By the song's end, the DJ was adamant that she stays to take a second turn. It was so tempting she might have even done it if it hadn't been for the sudden sensation of instinct that overwhelmed her.

Jade shook off the younger new acquaintance, who was busy saying how lovely her voice was. Despite never having spoken to each other before that night and only mingling for a few short hours, she asked for Jade's number, but Jade wasn't looking for a relationship. If she was, Jade could have just as easily done so when the scent of honeysuckle and cedar crossed her path. What allured this woman was what made it likely they'd never be more than what they were tonight. Appearances-wise, yes, many found her and other of her kin to be rather irresistible due to the stunning pure colors in their eyes, the flawlessness in most though not all, and much like herself after decades of proper attire and form a strong sense of independence in the modern life often intrigued people.

Stepping onto the street, she inspected the shades of the sky as if only realizing then how late it was. Under a light snowfall, she flicked on her jacket and made for her red stone townhouse. The smooth pavement that tapped under her steel-toe boots sounded much different nowadays than with cobblestone roads. The *thunk* of her shoe sent alley cats scurrying. At some point, one tap after another turned into two, and someone was clearly following her.

Jade kept walking along the well-lit road without looking back and feeling unfazed. Sure enough, the lit road eventually came to a darkened stoop with the dimmest porch light atop the stairs leading to the place she called home. Mere moments later, an arm wraps around Jade's throat, and a gun presses to her temple. The cool metal shook as it sat there, an act designed to scare anyone, yet Jade kept calm as she tried to understand why he was resorting to this. She knew he didn't want to be here deep down, whether it was money, food, or even anger-related. He didn't want to see how this ended.

"You sure this is what you want? There is no need for a gun. I can give you anything you want." She raised her arm to show the watch splayed across her pale skin. "Are you hungry?" As if directly answering, the man's stomach growls. "I see."

"Shut up. Give me everything on you." There wasn't even a hint of malice in his voice. He was desperate and pleading.

"I have nothing to offer you if you wish to pull the trigger. However, step back and enter the alley. I'll bring you some food and water, then forget you came here." A moment passes, and then the chilling metal lifts; his hold loosens around Jade, and his hands shove her as if to quickly push off towards the alley between her townhome and the one beside it. Intending to keep her word, she rummages through her cupboards for any canned food she might have. She had just moved and hadn't expected the need for a lot of food, but she did what she could. In one hand, she left with a warm plate of veggies and canned ham. A bag with enough food and water for a few days in the right hand.

After handing these over, she removed her leather jacket and gave it to the man; she had more. Being much skinnier than she imagined he'd be, it was obvious that the man would be cold. With this, she left and didn't look back. By morning, the man would be gone, and all corners of her home would be hers again. Ensuring to flick the front light off as she closed the door, her golden hazel eyes were the last to flicker in the night as she closed the door.

Destined Encounter

Hell's Kitchen sat quietly one late morning in November. Neighborhood kids racing each other to school and the wind whipping through the streets, not much was to be heard or seen as Jade walked through the city. That was if you weren't the type to think dark and cloudy was a perfect way to see the daytime life. Jade was used to seeing the city at night; now she might find the local bar closed and abandoned until much later, just the bar for a karaoke night actually.

The twenty-four-hour laundry mat had an entirely different crowd; the city didn't have shady figures during the day as if they had no other talents, and no hungry and homeless looking to do whatever it took to get through the cold nights. Thus, the pleasures of venturing out today. A street performer smiles as a small group forms to offer their attention. Even the diner down the road would be tempting to enter for a cup of coffee as it bustled busier during the day. Entering, the chill of the streets rushes in, and mostly everyone near the door looks up to watch the door close so they might get warm again.

Few booths were left, leaving Jade to sweep loose strands of brown hair behind her pale ear as she courteously took one of the open bar seats that were still available. Truthfully, Jade found more appeal in the aroma around her than the food options in front of her. When asked what she'd like, she requested a black coffee, the smell of the brew which held a bitter note mixed well with a faint second one; it was honeysuckle and cedar. Jade knew it was the reason for her intentional move to Hell's Kitchen, and almost found the source shortly after moving and now again in this diner. The mixture was not as well balanced as if the person was still there, but Jade could tell meditating on this alone could comfort her greatly.

At first, back when she was making a trip through the district, she thought the scent was everywhere. Whether the fragrance belonged to a worker or a patron was impossible to discern. Knowing it belonged to someone who was not there currently but was often made an impression though deep inside, something felt ready to turn the wheel of fate at any moment. After finishing the bitter coffee, she took one to go, paid, and walked about until she found a park.

This open field was filled with dogs and their owners or dog walkers. It was easy to tell while observing from a bench which was which. Sense of smell was not the only tell yet more accurate regarding clumsy people versus nervous walkers. The true tell was the body language between two connected by a bond.

Jade's gaze fell pinpointedly on that random guy who thinks his roommate's dog will get him a date as if to prove it wasn't that difficult to read total strangers. The chances of observing such an array of personalities and interactions on display were usually the rarity of day walking; in a state like New York, the weather was like this most of Fall into Winter. Honestly, it was more amusing than it should have been; however, it also made it just as clear who didn't care for their animals beyond money or ego. If a paper trail from taking up psychology wouldn't leave Jade feeling so exposed, she would have enjoyed going beyond reading people. ruefully she didn't; it would leave too many curious questions.

Working, eating, reading, and writing from home, while it is beneficial to keep things simple and even private, she had yet to create a balance of purpose and peace. It was relieving to have a day off to sightsee her new home instead of skulking through it under the moonlit sky. That, as it may be, didn't ever matter given the circumstances. Jade knew her existence was not ordinary; she had learned long ago that she should never linger anywhere long enough to leave a mystery in her wake.

The brunette finally headed home, aware that the cloudy weather was temporary. As the rain showered the city and the pavement became wetter with every step, she watched the gray sky fade away. The creeping sun showed from behind the highest cloud, creating a perfect rainbow that arced just over the houses of her neighborhood. Like a beacon, as if Jade was one to get lost, she was almost as familiar with the city as a native to it might be.

Taking in rays of color, she barely noticed the sting upon her neck. Gradually, it grew into a burning sensation to which she held the colorful image in her mind as she swiftly entered her home. Once inside, the curtains were already drawn closed so the pain would disappear entirely. Though the sunlight couldn't enter the house, the artificial lighting revealed her neat home with just a flick of the switch.

Unpacking was a breeze, quick as a whip even. However, it was taking longer than expected for work to send more parts for the orders that kept coming in. On the coffee table sat a pile of papers, meant to be in the home office, from her checking her equipment stock. Once they arrived, she could get back to work putting together computers. Until then, she had scooped up her papers, put them away, and left her office with a slight click of the door closing.

Beyond the main room, a ruckus could be heard near the kitchen. Jade didn't need to be closer to know it was from the cellar. She dimmed the unique lights as she entered to spot a small red and white fox sniffing around its tail low. Seeing her, though, it perked up.

"What are you doing, Cecile?" The white tip tail flicked almost happily as she picked her up. "I know it's been a crazy few days, but we are settled now...so in you go." She used the pen doorway, which was large enough to step in to place her next to her partner Dodger, primarily brown and red. Jade observed how Cecile had gotten out. It appeared to be by luck that playing around had moved one of their toys close enough to climb out. She'd have to make a cover to go with the expanded space for them. Bamboo bars came to mind, but for now, she moved the toy back, exited through the gate, and made her way over to her other pens. One with a pair of rabbits, like the foxes, they could be told apart by color and hints in the pattern.

The pair spent their time now separated since she was not ready for babies. Just beside the rabbits sat an empty pen temporarily as she didn't travel with her last duo of animals. There was a whole mountain of space for wild cougars at the previous place she had stayed with a good friend. Both the weather and area counted them out in this move. In Canada, where she lived before, bigger prey was much more accessible. Luckily, Jade had a small farm-like space in the back, just big enough for a pair of goats. At least Jade considered filling the third pen with them anyway. The fox and goats could have ramps or stairs with exits to the yard if she prepared it right, but she hadn't started yet; now she knew that would have to be done soon.

"Stay patient a little longer, guys. I'll get you fixed up tomorrow." As if they could understand her, they settled into a ball, tucked in some tail or leg they wanted to cover, and relaxed. She closed the door at the top of the stairs, latched it, and went to her computer. On other trips around the neighborhood, she hadn't seen any department stores, so she looked up a supply store open all night. While scoping the website for everything she needed, she was delighted to discover that she could purchase the items and simply pick them up, streamlining her shopping experience with minimal need to interact with others.

After several hours, she gathered her keys and left at sunset. The trip took twenty minutes with night traffic and pedestrians walking about. The hardware/24-hour convenience store took her name and offered to transfer everything into the back of the truck; not needing it, she turned them away and handled it herself. Making sure to appear to struggle a little bit plus still perfectly place everything where it would fit took some effort, but she quickly made her way home again. In the brief time she had left the animals alone, they'd gotten antsy.

The foxes came with her to the backyard after she moved all the wood and materials in the garage or through the gate and closed it again. As for the rabbits, she let one have the whole cellar while the other had more space once the divider was taken out. She tied up her shoulder-length hair, pulling it out of the way as she started preparing the project.

Cutting the wood would be too inconsiderate to her neighbors; it was now closer to 9 in the evening. So, any major work with tools would have to wait till a fitting time the next day. With that in mind, she dug and scooped, carving a path in the dirt until she reached the appropriate depth for each animal's pen, excluding the rabbits. However, she made a little commotion, self-chopping the small supports it would take to hold up the newly foundation-free sections hoping her neighbors wouldn't feel intolerant to the noise.

The cellar wall was still intact several feet above where the hole was to be made and then supported, after which she'd covered the holes with a better permanent door, so the fox didn't get out when returned to the pen. The next day, in her garage that sat below her living room beside the stairs that led to her front door, she began cutting the larger required wood with the door halfway up for airflow while dust flew around. She built the steps and re-prepared the paths carved out the night before, installing them into the supports she had made.

Both foxes were once again returned to the pen, and a bamboo bar roof was placed on top with hinges for easy opening if needed, but a latch too for their escape stunts. The rabbits were satisfied with their adventures when given but effortlessly went back to the same old setup once the time came to go back. She wouldn't dare leave them to their own devices too long as they were enough of a mess regularly, let alone what she had to clean when they were out and about.

The doors to each pen looked snug and even from either side, which was for the purposes of keeping them comfortable during cold weather and snowstorms. Jade expected the weather to bother them, being she hadn't let them out much when she was on the mountains as the lions, she tamed slightly, would not have hesitated to eat them up. She laughed, knowing the big cats she lured in with toys and treats would miss her, but they also had her friend to keep them company.

The townhome she owned now was lovely, spacious, and thankfully had a yard behind the property. The alleys beside her home were deceiving, but one led to her gated yard and the other to her neighbors. The width was not as lovely as how long it was. It went just over half an acre back. It wasn't expected in this part of town, next to all the traditional condos, lofts, and townhomes, this set of 4 townhouses at the end of the street had the same design as did another cluster on the corner further down the road that led to another lot of specific concepts. Some that did not have ample space behind had a roof balcony or a small pool. Forgoing the other options was ideal for Jade. Seeing as she owned it, she could do as she saw fit and was confident in her adjustments so far.

She left the cellar after admiring the pens and witnessing how comfortable the animals were; the rest of her day was devoted to work. Sometime between all the wood cutting and building outside and installing the bamboo top inside, a load of packages was left at her door. They covered the top stair and even the second. Taking boxes in two at a time, they eventually covered the floor of her office. It looked like Jade's first full day back would be the next day if she didn't speed things up, so she did.

What could have been a day spent organizing the parts pulled from the boxes quickly turned into a pile of connected computer parts or whole units growing in the corner of the room. Getting ahead of herself, Jade soon realized she would have to report half the pile today and control herself for the next few days. To ensure her pace seemed steady, never drawing attention, the moment she completed more than eighteen computers, it was time to walk away. Her attention gradually turned to her hunger, which would worsen if not managed. Of course, she hated doing anything to her little animals, but now was not the time to wait or feel bad.

Entering her cellar, she felt a thick tension as if they knew, and though used to it, they knew a little pain would occur for one of them. The last time had been Cecile, so she picked up Gump, a grey cotton-tail rabbit. He had a spiral of grey and white just on his hip joint, while Patty had an all-white coat with simple black specks around her feet. His jitters showed as he tried to jump free using her shoulder, though he was firmly in her hand. He wasn't going anywhere. The newly replaced top to their pen went down as she left Patty. In the cellar, under the stairs, sat a small bathroom she'd soundproofed before moving in. Once inside, she held Gump close to her gut as she sat on the toilet lid. Not having been used, she wasn't disgusted, but she realized then that another arrangement should be made within this room.

His fur stood as she drew her head back just before she massaged the roof of her mouth with her tongue. This caused the muscles to relax, dropping two pointed canine teeth so they were even longer. Sinking them in, Jade waited for his efforts to become paralyzed before drawing on his blood; softly caressing his head with her fingers, she fed. Not in many years had something made her take too much blood. Not since she regained her control from several drastic circumstances that backtracked all the hard work she had put into learning a new way to survive. Like every other time, she breathed and cleared her mind. Never drink too fast or hard. She sealed the bite mark and cleaned his stained coat in the tub. With this, she massaged the pain away and gave him as she did with all the others treats and nourishment for their help.

She softly picked him up when Gump began chattering over his food and pets. His tension faded now that her hunger no longer set off his instincts. Exiting the room to face the other trio always seemed to be the same unified expectation of their friend's death turned to glee, seeing their sudden return. By the time she needed another feeding, they would all practically forget.

After a well-timed feeding that coincided with her day's activities, Jade settled into the rhythm of her existence. Time seemed both infinite and fleeting as a week flew by, strangely enough, for a timeless being like herself when she kept busy with work, hobbies, and projects while around her home life out there in the world speeds on by. The weather had been bright and clear for New York in the early winter, too well-lit for another trip through town by day. During the day, the city was off limits, but she filled her sleepless nights at the bar with karaoke nights. Sometimes, she would enter; other times, the regulars who had come to know her by name would miss her singing all the while she was just on the roof of the building beside it.

Laying on her back, staring at the stars drowned out by the city lights, she'd almost find peace. Peace for her was not in the sky, but a single moment when, down the road a bit further, a dinner would change shifts. Still in the night and hidden from sight, she'd reveled in the alluring fragrance from a worker making their way home. Something about that honeysuckle and cedar scent made her remember simpler, more enchanting days if you looked past all the chaos at the time.

Back in Brooklyn, just before the Second World War ended when so often fighting in the street occurred, a building caught fire. For saving a couple trapped inside she was given safety in their company despite her unnatural nature. They ran a coffee shop with baked goods, so on the surface, nothing was different about this smell. It swam out to her, giving her tranquility once more in those innocent faces pulled to the front of her mind.

Truthfully, Jade wanted to regret how she began rarely visiting as they aged. She'd met and loved their kids through seven years before Jade knew she couldn't live there anymore. It was not long after leaving that Jade felt drawn to return to her homeland of Italy. At great risk to herself she wanted to help as many people as she could facing the crisis of the Holocaust, though not the name for it then.

It was unwise to be seen so many years later by the same people of that community when she returned to America. Old fears of being noticed for what she truly was didn't hesitate to emerge once more. She kept to herself far longer than she should have, but that did tend to happen for those bearing the fate of remaining timeless. Numerous times, too many to count now, the loneliness of her nature was a reminder of the life she lived. Much like now on this roof, the air was no longer swimming with honeysuckle or cedar, draining away old memories as the sky clouded over, and the purpose of the night was gone completely.

There was nothing to do at home after her short trips out but sit in bed and rest or write. So, she wrote, recalling a jaw-line, a shade of hair, or a voice from any number of people she'd met, all to compile the perfect details a writer needed to create characters. She described places from crumbled old chapels to mansions with fields of yellow and green. Throwing in subtle particulars from her past wherever they fit best. The true stories never took the page, but it was worth the effort trying to capture a moment regardless of the risk if anyone ever figured the pieces out.

When morning came, the clouds were thicker but not enough for a bit of early morning rain. The last day of the work week beckons her instead, so she fulfills its demands order by order until she is done. Using an average pace, she finishes thirteen computers. She documents eleven as completed and two as half-finished. She orders more parts and sets everything aside for delivery later.

Her body itches to get out and expend energy despite her inability to. She's not the only one. Though she can let the fox outside and the rabbits roam in the central part of the house with her, she can't get out herself. Getting out a few hours a week makes no difference; she wants to run.

That night, as the sun falls below tree lines, she travels in the shadows swiftly to High Falls, taking to the parks along the water over the highway and again into dark wooded areas. The lights of the roads and city would never appeal to her, but she knew their purpose. Every step of the way, she observed her surroundings to make sure no one noticed her, not wanting to be disturbed her first time back in so long. She anticipated trouble at any second until she reached the largely empty area of High Falls.

Water from the hundred-and-fifty-foot drop sounded like an echoed crash in the vast woods. The moon lit up the water and surrounding terrain, making the most obvious notion of how much had changed in a little over a century and a half. This place was a more significant reminder of her past than she expected, but the sweet image of a couple in love sharing the beauty they saw in this place crossed her mind as proof. Seeing her friends joy in nature led her to guide the nearby area to begin preserving the land.

The cool water no longer profited millers, and the terrain was no longer used for manufacturing wool or transporting coal. It had grown back to its charming ways once more. Tossing her shoes to the side as she stuck her feet in. The chill didn't faze her, though she paused from going any further as it almost seemed too easy to get in at the basin, so she was at the top looking out in no time. Even standing on a rock in the center of the fall, this seemed less natural, more human, to her. Turning around, she let the heels of her feet hang ungrounded. Her arms stretched out, feeling the wind across her skin. She cleared her mind and fell backwards as if the wind might carry her.

Thirty feet down, she slowly pivots her torso and then brings her legs to follow. Just about twenty feet above the water, her arms come forward to make a perfect dive. There is no clap or splash, just ripples in the water beyond the fall's contestant stream and noise. Eventually, the water stills near the edges. Several minutes pass with another chilling breeze lifting the water slightly into small waves. Gasping as she resurfaced, even though the air was hardly needed, it was worth the breath of crisp air after witnessing the stunning image beneath the water. What would take decades to replicate was settled there now. Fish, seaweed, and rocks of every color shimmering from the moonlight.

Laying back, she could see a beautiful sky exposed there with no city lights to drown the stars away. This was indeed the only way to relax as a vampire. Beauty was anywhere you looked if you found the natural side of it. She stayed there bobbing in the water until the early hours of dawn began to creep in. The sky would get too light to run back in a few short hours, so she started the silent run back to Hell's Kitchen.

Nearing her neighborhood, Jade found an empty place to calmly return to her home, but not before a quick stop at the local diner. Of course, she wasn't starting her day, but it was a great time as the sun began brightening the sky to grab a coffee. She expects the night shift to have changed so as not to personally run into the woman whose fragrance stirs something in her. Yet, as she sits down, that waitress is the one who greets her, causing Jade to freeze more in that moment than the chilly waters from earlier ever could have made her.

She was dry after all that running she did. No, this was the kind of freezing that struck her heart. Trailing her gaze upward, Jade could tell the clothes were uniform, distinguishing her short blonde side part-swept hair as her own unique style. As quickly as Jade acknowledged the woman's arrival, her gaze shot back to the seat she was taking, hoping that she did not appear too rude.

"Good morning, my name is Rosalina. I'll be your waitress. What can I get you?" While it felt like far too long internally, almost immediately, her voice responded.

"A hot coffee, please." A scribble later, the blonde she had yet to give a second glance up at decided to ask her something further rather than leave.

"We just made fresh apple, lemon, and blueberry breakfast cakes. Did you want to try one?" While uniquely perky, her voice eased Jade's shoulders from tense. Daring to look up again, Jade knew Rosalina would be smiling from her voice; the moment she did, she felt the urge to stare and become lost in those light ocean blue eyes but pushed on. Even as Jade's response came out, it started as a whisper cracking through an unnatural dryness in her throat due to the corner of Rosalina's lips turning to a grin, raising her cheeks to display a beautiful set of dimples.

"An apple one sounds great." With that, Rosalina left her alone looking like a timid woman to place her order. Reeling from the encounter, Jade mentally scolded herself, having never expected to meet with this lively woman. Jade had to admit, though, that the fragrance was so fresh whether Rosalina was gone or had stayed wouldn't have been any clearer. Now that this self-drawn line had been crossed, Jade wondered, could she keep herself from getting too close? The last time anyone struck her boundaries like this, circumstances and time made it, so there hadn't been anyone to return to.

"Here you are, one coffee and one apple cake. Any cream or sugar?"

"No, this is great. Thank you, Rosalina." Jade replies and sips her coffee, expecting her to leave. She did not; instead, as soon as the name passed her lips, Jade could hear the pace of the waitress's heart speed up. Intrigued Jade gives a soft hum and locks eyes with Rosalina. Instantly a wave of electricity spreads across Jades chest.

"Sorry, you're new that is all. I was wondering where you're from?"

"Yes, I'm new here. I like to travel, but my family once came from Italy. What about you?" She didn't need to know, as it was apparent from her accent, she was a New Yorker born and raised specifically near or around Queens.

"I spent most of my life in Queens, but some of my family is from Brooklyn, too." Rosalina says confirming Jades thoughts.

"Can tell, just wasn't sure which part." Jade adds telling herself this is what ordinary people do. While she could act bitter and force her away, she had no reason, nor did she want to. She knew all the reasons she shouldn't let the interaction linger to long but felt an appeal to the woman brewing inside.

"Yeah, it's stuck with me." Rosalina says speaking of her accent. "I can't tell where you're from, well, except from your face. That's meant to be a good thing, I swear." If Jade could blush, she would. Rosalina trips over her words quite adorably.

"I know what you mean. I never really been anywhere long enough to pick anything up accent-wise." Finishing her drink, she stands to leave with her cake. The morning sun is now peaking along the back wall, only slightly dimmed by morning clouds that held the promise of a flurry. Sliding a twenty on the table, she smiles before leaving and offers Rosalina her best wishes. "Have a good day."

At home, her day felt different, like something had changed her from the encounter. She almost hoped for another chance for their paths to cross, but as soon as she thought about it, she refused to spare another moment. Being twenty for an eternity was her own burden to bear. This Rosalina, she told herself, would be gone in the blink of an eye. Remorsefully, she worked harder, fixed up the house more, and stopped her rooftop visits near the karaoke bar for nearly three weeks before she had the guts to test this newfound urge for closeness.

2

Dark Alley

Glints of holiday lights were all across town on a night so close to Christmas, except thankfully on the rooftops. While it was still too early for most places in the city to close, it was an excellent time to find her calm place. Personally, Jade had never been aware of this type of problem before. This allurement she experienced with Rosalina was different than saving people and getting appreciation back.

It was even further than building friendships and family with other eternal beings. So, because she had no clue, she used caution laying on the roof that night. Using her leather jacket, she patted it into a pillow shape and laid down out of sight as usual. Looking up, she tried to fill her thoughts with other things than the task at hand. Centuries of living under the same stars, and though she knew them all, she couldn't possibly find the same comfort in them tonight. As she lay there, the casual sounds of the bar dug at her ears, the stench in the streets burned at her nose, and the surface under her back stung at her torso. Suddenly feeling too tense to be here, Jade decided she needed to go. She was unsure of what control she had over her instincts in this situation but imagined the tension meant the worst was still to come.

Slipping her jacket back on, she thought it might be better this way. Jade told herself she should leave now while Rosalina was running late. She knew the blonde often passed by on her way from work. Her natural scent of honeysuckle and cedar was often evidence enough.

Typically, Jade would let the comforting smell be lost to on the wind a few blocks down. She never sought out where Rosalina lived and never let herself linger for too long. All the temptation previously likely wouldn't make the moment any easier. Taking her leave, Jade cleared several rooftops to return home when she paused suddenly.

Tonight, of all nights, the blonde waitress calls out her departure and specifically hurried towards the alley intent on cutting through it. Jade couldn't move a muscle as she listened. In mere seconds, the only thing presently in mind was Rosalina. How she was late getting off but still seemed lively enough. A fresh bubble mint gum popped into the air as Rosalina snapped it between her teeth.

Seconds ticked on Rosalina's wristwatch as she passed a door for the bar in the alley

Beyond the door, a man slams an empty beer bottle on the bar countertop and makes his way to the door. Jade felt her hands clench nervously at the man's exit. The loud bang sound caused Rosalina's heart rate to speed up and herself to stay, intent on seeing Rosalina make it clear to the other side. Jade asked herself why she was so afraid of this woman as her body stirred with some unknown instinct.

Deep down, Jade knew it to be a protectiveness. She wanted to be down there walking with her, but as she wasn't, she concentrated on the man she knew liked to piss outside. Thanks to all the alcohol, his inhibitions were already lowered. He stumbles before staring down the dimly lit alley. Licking his lips instantly in response to the sight of a young lady in the narrow alleyway; no matter who it is, his interest is apparent.

Even from five rooftops away, Jade can see Rosalina observe him over her shoulder as he begins bobbing his head to the music and walking towards her. Each swaying step he took began unsettling her, so she started walking faster. The more she pushed into the alley, the closer she came to Jade, but it was hardly fast enough since he was soon caught up and close behind her. By the looks of it, he was taller, or maybe it was her tight jeans that made her easy to catch. Regardless of the distance and the alley's pitch-black spots, one of which the pair had just entered, Jade knew Rosalina was scared.

"H..." He belched. Once his rancid breath reached Jade, it made her want to gag. "Hey, pretty! What's your name?" No answer came, just the footfalls that led to the next moment's scuffle where the blonde readies a fist, the sound of material stretching painting a picture for Jade. Rosalina seemed capable, so while half of Jade felt if Rosalina just walked faster, she'd be fine, the other half thought that the blonde might regret taking the alley. Though Rosalina seemed concerned about being in the darkest part of the alley, the sound of this guy's feet or foul stench was strong enough she didn't need to look back. The ghastly smells might have drilled through Rosalina as surely as the cold weather could if her focus wasn't more on getting further away.

The alley smelled of vomit, but this man's breath alone made Rosalina's chest stutter. Peering into the shadows, Jade swallows thickly at seeing Rosalina appear dazed or ill-prepared for his grip that spins her; the momentum helps when her fist collides with his head. Hearing the clash makes Jade want to intervene, but her principles hold her back. Startlingly to both women, it hurts him but not enough to knock him out or allow her to run. As he stood before her this time, Rosalina held her breath to avoid being caught off guard again.

What if she stepped in revealing abilities, and Rosalina could handle this guy. Jade asked herself before readying to leap another roof but couldn't get the guts to leave further. This time, an impact against what had to be the alley wall and a gasp of pain makes Jade drops her stance, stopping any attempt at leaving, securing Jade with full intentions to help if this escalates more. A distinct sound of bones creaking followed the brief yell.

"I said, what's your name? Bitch!" Through the beer breath and the nearly shattered bones, Jade could imagine her reason for not answering, but finally, the waitress gave her name.

"Rose- my name is Rosalina."

"What was that?" He snarled as if he didn't get a good enough answer because of her frightful tone. "No one is here to save you, so just do what I say."

At this, a struggle broke out. Rosalina was kicking and fighting to get away. The tearing of her clothes told Jade this was getting out of control; immediately, Jade made for a closer roof and another. With several more attempts, Rosalina tried and probably could have gotten away if a knife wasn't just drawn and pressed to her. If the swift 'click' sound and sudden lack of struggle were anything to go by Jade need end this.

Not smelling any blood, she pushed aside her hesitation and quietly crossed to the last roof. It was too late as Jade towered over the ledge across the devious scene. Rosalina boldly kicked the man in the groin, expecting him to fall in pain, but instead, he cupped himself with one hand and held the knife even closer to her with the other. Not as affected as someone not wearing a guard would be, he gave a frustrated growl and lunged his body into hers. Colliding their shoulders and letting the blade sink into her stomach before letting go, he seemed satisfied. Blood filled Jade's senses as the squelch of the knife tore open skin. He had enough of the struggling or didn't like the look of disgust in Rosalina's eyes.

"Shit." She muttered; moments later, Jade landed from above quietly behind him. After letting go of the blade, he fixes his slouched shoulders and grabs for the buckle of his cargo pants. Jade yanked him up by the scruff of his wood-dusted shirt, throwing him against the wall behind them. Hard enough that wasting time to make sure he wasn't getting back up wasn't needed, but knowing it was just light enough, he'd make it through the night.

Rosalina held her abdomen wound as she slipped down the wall in shock. She was not focused on Jade or what she'd done because, while obviously, the man was not there anymore, she looked down, too shocked to decide what to do. Rosalina was more worried about the knife than who or how the man was stopped.

"Don't take the knife out," Jade said, getting close enough to see the amount of blood beginning to soak her white tank top and trench coat. Having wasted enough time debating the risks before, more or less straightening out her responsibilities over her desires and fears, she scooped up the blonde, careful not to jostle her too much.

"Don't worry, I'll take you home."

"What? Home? I need to go to the hospi-" Unable to finish, Rosalina fainted due to current blood loss.

"Trust me, there is nothing they can do for you now." Not wanting to let the situation worsen, Jade promptly leapt to the rooftop and ducked when she heard the side door to the bar open.

"Come on, man, you were supposed to be pissin'! Whoa, what happened to you?" A younger, definitely- still drunk companion says, not expecting to find said friend on the floor of the alley. Knowing the unconscious man had someone to get him, she fled, not making a sound. Crossing roof after roof as lightly as possible so as not to spill more blood by jostling the knife, Jade leaves the busy bar behind. Her feet fall just a bit heavier with Rosalina in her arms. Nothing could distract her from safely getting them to her home instead of possibly being exposed to anyone still in their homes this late at night.

Jade tested her footing on the edge of the shingles next to her townhouse before jumping risks aside to the ground near her office window that pointed into the alley. The jump did exactly as Jade was trying to avoid causing Rosalina to pale even more. Panicking, she climbed through the window, disregarding the papers or nicknacks she'd knocked on to the floor, and took Rosalina into the living room. Jade placed her on the sofa before gathering the items she needed. Rags, bandages, and water.

Deciding to pull the knife out now meant a lot of the time left for Rosalina would be lost. Taking it out wouldn't help keep Rosalina alive, but then again nothing else could help her either; Jade could do only one thing. Accessing the rough placement and unknown depth with any internal issues, Jade decided it was now or never. So, she readied herself and pulled the knife out.

Jade rolled the hilt between her fingers before swiping the long switchblade deeply across her fingers and palm, appearing as if trying to clean it but purposefully doing entirely the opposite. Laying down the blade, her now free hand spread the layers of skin. Jamming her own bloody fingers inside, she felt the seriousness of the wound. Jade's instincts told her this wasn't going to heal her, but she kept hope that in using her blood, Rosalina would be healed, not change.

Jade applied more pressure against her palm to keep the flow going. Rosalina needed more to recover; however, so far, she'd lost twice as much as Jade could give. Unavoidably, Jade removes her fingers to watch the hole close. What's done is done now, though it didn't sit right just yet that she was now making another being immortal. Unlike her own change by doing nothing sooner, the options and choices were removed for the lifeless woman before her. The heartbeats faded to a stop now, but her skin was still warm, plump, and covered in blood. Doing what she could, Jade cleaned up and moved her now guest to her bedroom on the second floor. Waking up and giving answers wouldn't happen so soon; it was better Rosalina rose comfortable and that Jade be ready to answer any questions. One rule she and many immortals follow is never willingly leave a trace. Returning to the alley was a must, as was eating to replenish what was given. Traces of the incident were there, with Rosalina's blood on the ground, which had to be treated with a mixture of peroxide and lemon she'd brought from home. Skin tissue from the man was stuck in the wall, but it was irrelevant, so she left it. After a double look around, Jade was sure everything was fine as it was now. The one thing outside of karaoke night she liked about this bar was that the cameras in the front were the only ones that worked. One was at the side, but it wasn't sending any feed or power. It should be working for anyone else's sake, but it was a fortunate benefit for tonight.

She tucked her cleaner out of sight beneath her jacket and walked calmly from the alleyway as stragglers were exiting out the front slowly due to closing time. They joked about the unconscious drunk found in the alley earlier and how he was babbling on about some blondie. Jade took their jokes as a clear sign no one believed him, or if they did, he simply had his ass handed to him by a lady. Served him right, even though he did deserve worse.

Returning home, she checked in on Rosalina. Seeing the light skin gleam paler, Jade resigned to only stay momentarily. This wasn't how she expected her night to go, especially once she decided not to risk an encounter when stressed. There was much to be glad hadn't happened, like losing her temper at someone hurting Rosalina, but plenty she felt could have gone so different.

What bothered her the most was that she couldn't decide if this had all happened because of the connection to Rosalina or if the events were already in motion before tonight. Her friends would say it's not one or the other. That every moment is a reaction to a million years of interactions reaching the present. A feeling of foreboding sat in Jade's gut as she wondered about the consequences of her becoming a maker.

Pushing off the door frame, she sighed, not usually one to use unnecessary sound effects, but found that she still could not get her nerves settled. In the hushed darkness of the room, the burgeoning affection towards the recently encountered stranger whispered to Jade until she broke the vulnerable stillness by turning on the bed-side lamp and ensuring the curtains were fully closed. It was so unlike her to wait idly when she'd already put off feeding long enough, she thought to herself as she entered the cellar to find the four animals were almost none the wiser of the changes upstairs. To them, all that matters is the predator and the prey instincts they felt with her entrance, and the difference when she left Dodger with Cecile again was noticeably calmer.

She busied her idle hands with an hour of work but eventually sent an email asking for the day off as she wasn't feeling well. She was fine but couldn't put one more CPU on another motherboard with everything going on. Usually, challenging mental work would have been enough to subdue the churning thoughts; on this occasion, she needed a more direct way. She took the time to open the pen door leading outside before too much light crossed her home and decided to begin working on some writing.

Dancing a story through a time in history she'd been party to, so readers feel connected to the scenario but not so much so that she'd be found out was her passion. Ever since childhood, she'd wanted to create books that children or adults could love. In those days, once a child hit a certain age, they just worked. No one had time for frivolous things if you didn't have the right circumstances in your favor from birth.

Of all the pages she had written out thus far, nothing came to mind for her to continue them. Was it her relatable history to the pain Rosalina would be enduring? The fire in her veins the way it would turn to ice soon enough. It couldn't have been the deception clearly drafted between them. Rosalina unknowingly crossed paths with an immortal while Jade knew of her connection and had seen Rosalina for some time from afar, but that wasn't why she'd done this.

Try as she might to picture the toiling seas of her past, fires littering battlefields, or villages celebrating freedom, anything to help, she could only recall the events in the alley and the spilled blood. Thumping her table in frustration, Jade starts pacing her office. This was no way to introduce herself as a maker. No way to confess everything. She needed to think and not with the reminders lingering in the air.

With the daylight, the waterfall wasn't an option, so she lay on a sofa in the basement. She placed beating music in her ears and closed her eyes to center herself. The house was small enough that any noise should get her attention. Closing her eyes, a sudden pulling feeling came over her as uncontrollable as hypnosis, like falling into a deep pit of memories she had once given up looking back on so long ago.

* * *

Jacopa smelt a familiar old, damp, borderline foul well in her home city of Florence like it was yesterday. She ran the same mundane errands for her parents growing up. Travel to the well before the sun colored the sky. Almost always, when she arrived, there would be a small line like today to drag water from the well. Today was hotter than all the other days in summer, but she did not need to rest before heading home, nor did she have the time.

Her sweet mother had a fire lit when she returned. Looking at her with the fire lighting and coloring strands of greying hair would be misleading to an outsider. The only difference between them, separate from the fifteen years, was the dark hair and brown eyes she got from her father. Otherwise, her nose that flared when angry, strong jawline, and prominent cheekbones sat the same on her face as it did her mother's. To Jacopa, while still looking youthful, her mother was thirty-five and was beginning to show it.

Jacopa left briefly to feed the animals and do rounds before break-fast. Some of the yard needed hard labor as piles of dung sat in mud, ruining the little amounts of grass the pigs had in their pen. After having some oats, she needed to tend to this, but her mother called out as she went to leave. Having probably heard her cleaning her bowl, Jacopa stops the scrapping of wood and the splashing of water to hear.

"Jacopa, I need you to take your father his tools. He left them in the other room. Hurry before he gets there and tries to make his way back." He couldn't just leave; she was sure he'd need to pay for more tools from someone supervising. Her father had taught her so much about the trade even though she couldn't work in it. She hurriedly grabbed his hammer and other carpenter tools as she thought of where she could find him. He was tearing down a former shop someone bought, or was he now working on the bridge, she wondered momentarily. Knowing that her mother would be off tailoring in her grandparent's old shop, she wouldn't see her when she returned.

"I'll see you around for supper, Ma." She called out as she left. Out of breath after running all the way to the shop that her father might have been working on to discover he wasn't there was a little off-putting, but she was hopeful to catch him at the bridge; he wasn't running, even though now she'd gone in the wrong direction. Her father told her that using stone was a new concept; still, she imagined he enjoyed making something important to the city. When she arrived, she saw the beautiful structure only just being started. Some supports were in place, but that was nearly it so far. Finding her father talking to a tall man with crossed arms, she called out before he gave the man anything.

Her father was a peppered-looking man who was built for the work. First, she had to lower her gaze from them in a respectful bowing manner; she then immediately looked only at her father as he proudly beamed at her for bringing him precisely what he had forgotten. How he had, she didn't know, but he thanked her and kissed her forehead before returning his attention to the other man. He begged for his forgiveness before guiding her away.

Her legs were slowly burning as she walked with him down the side of the bridge to a tree. He told her to sit a little while, catch her breath, and watch how the work was done if she wanted before heading home. He then gave her some coins for the trip and to grab something later on her way back. It wasn't much, but enough for a loaf of bread or some juicy fruit. Only sitting for a short while, she made her way through town at a much different pace, stopping occasionally to see something of interest. What she really wanted was clean water and some fruit.

As she reached out for a peach, a hand grasped her wrist. The fingers on her were dirty and led to a trembling young child. Jacopa was sure the child would already be blistered up from the heat if she hadn't had a dress and a blanket-like cloth draped around her. A whisper from the weak voice begged for coin. The hand then let her go as clearly, she'd gotten her attention. Jacopa pulled the coin pieces from her pocket and handed them to the child, hoping she could use them better. After the tiny hands had the money, A fragile but raspy cough that echoed her suffering beckoned the shopkeeper's attention.

"Oi! Get out of here, you filthy thing. Sorry, ma'am. I hope you didn't waste your coin on the poor child. She looks like death is coming for her." He said, making some attempt to salvage a sale. She walked away, not bothering to explain that what mattered was that perhaps that money might bring that girl from the brink of starving and to better health. Making it back home before the sun rose above their home, she wiped her face along the cuffs of her sleeves and then quickly started on the chores that needed doing. Several hours later, Jacopa had to roll her sleeves up as she felt increasingly hot. Exhausted even as only a third of the day had passed.

Being used to working in this heat, she wondered if the running had made her more spent. She worked on the fencing where a flock of sheep was kept by moving them to an alternate pen. One had a bad habit of nudging the fence as it walked by; occasionally, it had to be re-dug, straightened out, and packed full of dirt again. Filth had layered her arms by the time she finished; this time, she wiped her-self down with a wet cloth and decided to lay down for a short while.

Not feeling well enough to get up again and have dinner, she told her parents she hadn't the energy; they must have realized her work in the yard because they let her be. Before she knew it, she grew restless yet completely sore at some time in the night. Thinking perhaps she hadn't had enough water that day, she climbed out of bed, drew a cup full, and soundlessly crept back to bed. The effort left her too clammy to cover up, making her even more uncomfortable.

Jacopa greeted her parents the following day through her door, the lack of her presence warning them she was unwell. They couldn't get sick knowing full well with one down, even for a day, they would suffer. She told them she was probably overworked; in response, they made her swear to go to the doctor soon if it kept up too long.

That day, oats and water were left at her door. She ate half and fell back, unable to move beyond having a drink here and there. The following day, after no sleep from a dry throat and aches, a wave of energy gives her the strength to get dressed and go to the doctor. She needed this to be over quickly to tend to the food they grew and the numerous things their animals required.

It became unclear when she woke up next what was happening from one moment to the next. She'd made it to the doctor but must have dropped right in their doorway as everything hurt more, especially her knees. She heard a few mumbled words from the doctor. She called out her parent's names at seeing his face and watching him bring a dark mask to his face before walking over. "They haven't got it... They need to know." His assistant was ushered off with the task of retrieving them. This mask was all she needed to know what her future looked like, but whenever her body spared her, she tried to speak with the doctor. Asked how she could have gotten something worse than a cold? He was just as perplexed due to a spike in cases lately. So, he asked her many times if she remembered anything. All she could get out was "a poor girl," which she thought made no sense; still, he nodded from the foot of her bed. She was separated from others and asked to try to cough into the cloth he gave her.

Once her parents arrived, the broken look they gave said the one thing she hadn't been told. How bad it was and that she wasn't going to get better. The doctor gingerly spoke to them about her. Finally, he admitted he didn't have anything that might help now. Being exhausted and overworked must have made her more susceptible. Her father gently put a book on her bedside, then looked at her with tear-filled eyes and a wobbly lip before ushering her sniffling, grief-stricken mother away.

Over the kind words the doctor gave her about them being symptom-free and him not recommending staying long, she could hear her mother's grief melt away as she began fussing about all the work that would need to be done without her. That short gaze from her father and slight sniffle from her mother was their good-bye. She couldn't pick up the book, but she knew it was one he once read to her as a child. A subtle reminder that she was his little girl.

More and more, the moments next blurred by. Until Jade was unsure how long ago it was that her parents left her and how long ago it was that she saw the doctor leave. Eventually, Jacopa looked out to the night sky, not expecting to see opal-colored eyes across the way; struggling, she went to sit up, and they were gone. Thinking her mind was playing tricks, hallucinating about creatures she knew didn't exist. Only in her book were they real. Jade thought fondly of her book and how father told her these stories to make her brave and strong, not to scare her.

Slumping back down, she gave a groaning cough. She flicked her eyes to the same place until morning. If she closed her eyes to sleep, she didn't realize it until it was a new day; aside from being given water, she was left alone. Feeling chills and fever, occasionally, she might feel better long enough to smell an odd spicy mixture. The doctors told her it was to keep the other patients from getting sick. It was apparent the doctor struggled to keep up with his other patients, let alone cater to her, so he left his assistant to scramble about; even with curtains around her and a few others, Jacopa could sense he would rather be doing his job out there than risk exposing himself in closed off quarters with them, when others who arrived before her began dying, Jacopa resigned that she couldn't stop herself from following. No matter how much she wanted to get better.

If only she could survive somehow, she thought, and as the thought crossed her mind that night, a whisper crept into her ear. It gave her chills, but no fever followed, as it clearly said.

"Anything for a cure." Looking around, a slimmer shadow than the doctor or his assistant appears against the curtains.

"Yes." She cracks out the dryness in her throat, ignoring the sting.

"I'd give anything to survive." This time, the shadow slips to her bedside like a dream.

"No more pain, no more cold or heat, and no more tiredness and hunger?" Like a question before greeting the afterlife. Her grim reaper, she realized, was waiting for her to answer.

"Yes." She accepted this fate; her mind told her it was time in a way she might welcome it, like her old stories.

"Present your name."

"Jacopa Di Fazio." Suddenly, the shadows melted away, showing a man fully clothed in a priest's attire, his jaw-length curled hair fitting the charade, but as he was grinning slyly, she felt a falseness to his appearance. Jade tensed in surprise at how awake and alive she feels when he takes her arm with a freezing hand. He bites the underside of her arm, and a numbness takes over her immediately. A cry falls shy of escaping her lips. He then tears his palm open, dripping his blood into her mouth. Closing, it leaves the taste of liquid dusty metal that slides down her throat despite the urge to throw up. Without a sign of remorse, he licks his hand before swiping his tongue over her torn skin.

"And by fate, we meet." He slips her arm underneath the blanket and fades into the night as burning fills her veins. Through the pain, she begins to question whether the vision of him was even real. Was her head offering something it couldn't provide, or was this something else entirely she had allowed? Her breathing became shallow as the sun rose.

The doctor's shock at her inability to move or speak spread to his eyes before he could express any audible disbelief. Upon seeing signs of blood, he swiftly closes the curtains, gives her water, and cleans her up but says nothing more can be done. He too has resigned her to her fate and leaves her alone from then on; not even his aid checks on her except to see if she has passed on. The fiery pain goes on till night. Then a slipping, fading feeling comes; she knows this is where the end is. Closing her eyes, her heart stops, her chest fails to rise again, and she's greeted by the same voice from the night before.

Still speaking in a whisper, he bids her a welcome. Suddenly, she can move and sits up to find no stiffness or pain. The fire has turned to ice, but even that is slowly creeping away. Feeling fixed, she couldn't thank him enough; as she spoke, she heard a shuffling across the floor beyond the curtains, and chills crawled over her skin instantly. The assistant brought his head through with his mask, growing startled to see her up.

The next thing she knew, her body sprang toward him, grasping his shoulders out of hunger. She felt the urge before she could even think what to say that would make him run. This hunger was different; it wasn't in her stomach but throughout her whole body.

Her chest was searing with rage and disgust, but she sank her teeth into the man without even realizing it and drank his blood. She coughed once she let go. He was gone, never even having a chance to scream.

"What have you done to me?" Jacopa asks, taking to swirling her tongue in her mouth and collecting the metallic fluid to spit a glob of blood at the ground between them. Instantly, her body sprang erect, and her fury calmed as she convincingly thought that was an insulting way to act.

"Just what you wanted. I made you immortal. You are cured of death. Come as your maker. I'll show you more, so much more."

* * *

This echoes in her ears as she opens her eyes, returning her mind to her home on the couch in the basement. Somehow, she had been buried in her memories well into the night. Her instincts and senses told her so. Getting up, she pulled the earplugs out and listened as she headed upstairs. A scuffle against the trash bins beside her house and a panicked heartbeat reached her ears.

Speeding through the house to her room, she sees the bathroom window open. Mentally pleading it's not Rosalina, she slips her head out to see. Knowing the initial impulse is too strong to ignore. Even if she had understood it then, she'd been changed; there was no time to stop her. Just as she had been shocked at twenty years old, Rosalina now would be, too.

3

The Incident

The attack in the alley was over; that was all the darkness told her. It wasn't that she didn't feel the fire in her body; the burning sensation was all over her skin, not just where the blade had gone in, but it was ebbing away. Besides that, her head reeled, trying to sort it all out. The soft surface beneath her back said she was not stuck dying against the wall. Like a clouded memory, she did remember a woman helping her and then offering to take her home, not the hospital; this beckoned questions about the reality of her situation.

Time seemed to slow as one hand reached to feel for the wound. The pain that didn't come at touching the area only added further questions. As she lay there perplexed, the fire before began to feel chilled. Like goosebumps except inside, making sitting up feel less slow and pained.

The room around her looks unique, like a mini museum, as she searches for a mirror but finds none. Her feet padded almost silently over the floor, each step bringing her closer to exiting the room; only then could she see a bathroom from the doorway. Flicking the light on, she faces the mirror. Something looked off, but she glimpsed over her body to her abdomen.

Frightened at the sight of no hole beneath the one in her shirt, she patted it and prodded her fingers at the skin, but nothing. Looking hadn't changed anything; the blood on her shirt was dried, and the stab was gone. Just as she went to exit in a huff to find this mysterious woman, a noise caught her attention.

One usually would ignore something as minor as someone kicking a bottle across the pavement, but her ears heard it, and then she also picked up a cough. Drawn to the window, she slid it open and inhaled, feeling a breeze blow in her face. The icy goosebump sensation spread just before an unnatural kind of hunger filled her mind.

As the man sits behind the trash bins and lays a blanket over his legs, she feels herself moving closer, leaning out. It doesn't register for her until both feet are particularly wedged between bricks and her fingers dig into the wall that she is outside, climbing closer to this man.

He smells as homeless as he appears, but it doesn't matter as she hangs just above him. A sharp prick forces her mouth open, but what it was precisely evades her as a blur of things occurs. She is on top of him after a slightly surprised, scared Yelp escapes him. His heart is racing, the bins are banged, and the struggle stops. The icy sensation dissipates, and a pair of hands grab her firmly.

Licking her lips, Rosalina feels a slick liquid drip; her hand catches it. Drips swell into the cupped hand, filling the palm instantly. Rosalina didn't need to see it to know the metallic taste in her mouth was blood. She wants to scream but doesn't so as not to make the situation worse, and instead looks at the woman with panic racing through her.

"What...? How...?" she can't get the right questions to come out. The familiar woman tells her to take a deep breath. The panic, however, doesn't disappear as she finally realizes that under the hand on her chest, her heart isn't pounding. When she does exhale, she bends over, needing to puke.

"Oh no! over the cans." She's told, and strangely, she lets herself be guided to them. It's not a lot, despite the disgust she knows she feels. "Let's get you inside." Again, she follows. She wants answers. No, she needs them. "Sit a moment. I have to go deal with..." she trails off, not wanting to remind her. Her eyes are a soft, familiar amber; it must be the reason she decides to listen to her.

A few minutes later, the woman enters the room again, bringing in a strong lemon and peroxide smell. Setting a spray bottle down, the dark-haired woman sits in a chair near her, clapping her hands on her legs as she does so. She looks woeful at first but casts this aside as she adjusts her gaze to her.

"My name is Jade. You work at the diner down the road. I... You were attacked." Jade, the name buzzes in her head, and then it clicks why she looks so recognizable.

"You were that lady from a while back! I was attacked, but there's not even a scar. What's going on?" Her eyes look furious. "You brought me here, not a hospital! What is wrong with you!? Are you a doctor?"

"No."

"Then what the fuck! You couldn't have fixed that by yourself. What the hell was all that out there? What have you done to me?" Rosalina lashed out, stressing the beds of her fingers while wringing them over the hems of her bloody clothes.

"Is it okay if I call you Rose?" Jade asks calmly. Initially Rosalina bristles at the thought of a nickname. Despite her family always trying new ones the only one that ever stuck was Rosie and only her cousin used it. Hearing the name Rose cross Jades lips though sounded refined and enticing. Feeling relaxed but unwilling to show it, Rosalina crosses her arms giving Jade a single nod to get answers.

"Well, Rose, it's a bit of a story. I am a... Vampire. I couldn't just heal you. You lost too much blood by the time I got you out of there. I didn't want to do something like this without permission, but I gave you my blood to help you heal. You could say I had hoped you would heal before you bled out. We wouldn't exactly be here, I guess." Despite just taking her seat, Jade begins pacing by the windows. "I've never transformed anyone before. Normally, you need someone to teach you. None of this went as expected, so I understand if you want to leave. If by chance you want to stay, I'll answer anything you want to know."

Watching the waves of emotions cross Rosalina's face made fear drip cold from Jade's heart. Under the pressure of the blondes' fist-clenching hands, the silence was disrupted with a slow creaking of bones. Jade didn't dare to speak a word as the strain went on. Rosalina takes a deep breath before beginning with her retort.

"So, I died...just died." As Rosalina says this defeatedly, Jade feels an aching loss strike her. "Does anyone or everyone know? You made me a vampire. Just how long ago was the attack?" It is always a lot to take in, but at least she's talking, no longer yelling, Jade thinks.

"Roughly twenty-four hours ago. I got you out of the vicinity of the incident before anyone saw." Jade says, trying to give some hope of returning to as regular of a life as possible.

"Where were you? You didn't stop me from hurting that man." She was shaking, causing Jade to stand still to confess.

"I... I'm sorry. I laid down to center myself, to prepare for you to wake up. Then I don't know. I was vividly remembering my own change and came out just as you fed on him. It's likely the same instinct I had when changing your first feed is completely out of your control. My maker sabotaged my choices, so I intended to show you my way first, but I failed."

"What's your way?" Her voice was softer now, and her eyes turned more curious.

"Animals. With enough training, you can stop before you take too much. It does take time to learn, but it's possible." At this, regret crosses Jade's face. "I don't mean to assume you'd stay."

"I can't go home. I don't really have anyone to return to, but I can't leave. What if I, as crazy as all this is, take someone else's life but in public? What if I get caught? I need to be taught. I never would have guessed this kind of thing would be possible, but now that it is happening, I...I can't regret it. You saved me in a way, so thank you."

"What." Jade blinks in shock that she is so willing to accept this life.

"Tell me everything. I saw you that one morning, so daytime is okay, right? Like some of it is a myth or something?"

"Why aren't you upset still? You just got told the most outlandish thing and you are more curious. You seemed in a hurry from work... are you sure no one is expecting you?" Jade looked away slightly, knowing she didn't need to ask the last question.

"To be honest, I had a date. I tried to put it off by working late, but my boss told me to get going and not be late." Rosalina bites her bottom lip in Minor embarrassment. "Still, I always wanted this as a kid. The fantasy, not the blood and killing. It happened, well happening, and I know I am disgusted by what happened not just out there but at the bar, too. It's not fair that I got hurt, no killed, and he is what? Still breathing? At least I have processed I have no stab wound and no heartbeat. Even though both were frightening to realize, you...you helped me. I've always processed things fast, so I move on fast. It's a bad habit, but if I keep it positive, it's not so awful."

"Oh." It's Jade's turn to feel embarrassed. Telling herself she shouldn't have yelled. "Guess I reacted differently to my change." Relieved that Rosalina was being so reasonable after worrying the blonde might react like she had when learning the truth, she took a seat again. It was decided the moment Jade knew this was coming, she wouldn't force Rosalina to endure a century under her thumb as her maker did. "You will learn a lot by doing, feeding, and resting. Though you won't sleep, you will find it nice to close your eyes occasionally. The best place to start is probably not the beginning, but I'll share everything I know. We can discuss history some other time."

Jade shared for a brief while about their abilities and downsides. This led to more questions, making the fact that they could do or hear almost anything slightly irrelevant as more information passed between them. The fact that Rosalina accepted that sun and silver were just vulnerabilities while decapitation and stakes were final so easily made Jade wonder if Rosalina was more ready for this new life than anyone she'd met before.

A whole new life that starts in darkness and isolation. It beckoned all the worst people naturally, but here Rosalina was an innocent, looking to her to give her a fresh start. While she explained the risk of her returning to work, Jade mentally wondered what the final straw would be. Not being able to go back to work for a bit, making sure her family never knew, or eventually, they'd have to leave and have new identities.

Learning any of that wasn't easy for Jade if she was to tell the truth. Still, she focused on the now as she spoke to remind herself, she was going to be different than her own maker. After all the need-to-know stuff, she let Rosalina have a moment to call her job and give them some excuse to miss work for a few weeks or more. Meanwhile, Jade rounded up Patty in a cage to show Rosalina how to control a feeding and how to feel the energy left in an animal or person depending on what came of Rosalina's preference after practicing.

Entering the living room again, Rosalina eyed the rabbit silently, giving an occasional yes while listening to her boss on the phone. Jade set the cage down on the coffee table just as Rosalina told her boss, as if reiterating that after being attacked last night, she probably needed some time before coming back in. Clarifying that the day shift still wasn't something she could do; after what happened, she just needed time to get past it. A few weeks at most, promised Rosalina, ending the call.

"I'm not sure how much we can prepare you in two weeks," Jade admits after Rosalina hangs up. "Everything I can teach you I taught myself but had to do some of it in secret, which took a long time."

"I know, but if they wait that long, I might be able to get more time later. I'm sure they will let me know if they don't want me back. My family can always loan me a better reference."

"Your family does the food industry, too?" Jade voiced her question as a glint of fascination crossed her eyes as if Rosalina might tell her a familiar story. Jade couldn't help thinking a kind independent person like Rosalina would only leave home if they were not very nice people. "Why'd you leave?"

"Oh, four generations all similar but different. My move here was to learn the trade, not from family, to learn what they haven't tried. My grandma Jeanne passed away five years back; she wanted me to make us bigger." Jade saw a flicker of doubt in her prodigy but said nothing as she continued. Every detail seemed to ignite a spark of curiosity within Jade akin to discovering an old book with a trove of new mysteries in its pages. "Granted, I know they still won't approve of my lifestyle and choices," she continued, "so maybe they won't help me."

"If you throw in something about your Gran, I'm sure they respect her enough if they are still in the same work. First, before any family or friends, let me show you something. This is Patty. I know you just fed, but being new at all this, seeing her might make you hungry. This time, you should have more control."

"Oh, I don't want to hurt your pets."

"They aren't pets. They deserve to be treated like it with how much they help me, but they aren't. Patty hasn't been fed off of in a while, but before I let you hold her, let's reflect on your feelings. Then we'll get into what to do next, but please don't feel bad if Patty looks hurt after. I normally have a better system, but there isn't enough space downstairs for both of us."

"I feel that icy sensation again. Not like before, but it's like- " Rosalina said finding it hard to describe out loud for the first time.

"Goosebumps? That's your instinct. Listening to it sometimes will protect you, but in terms of feeding, it's in overdrive for now."

"How long can it take to have better control?" She wasn't looking anywhere except the rabbit. The words thankfully came out; as far as Jade could tell, it was a struggle.

"Honestly, I wouldn't know personally. I never saw anyone ignore their instinct and impulses. I'm not proud. It took me up to a century to leave my clan and start up on my own. I fumbled for a while, but with willpower, I changed a lot that was drilled into me." Hearing this, Rosalina's gaze flickers from Patty towards Jade as if suddenly needing to show she was listening. Once the truth was said aloud and a shared pause filled the moment with an unexpected closeness between them, Jade hurriedly breaks Rosalina's lingering focus on her by explaining their next steps. "If you palpate the roof of your mouth with your tongue, the muscles contracting the fangs in will give." As they released, Rosalina inspected them with her fingers, her touch curious and probing. It dawned on her then that was what pricked her mouth that first time.

Neither Jade nor Rosalina despite her self- inspection missed the way Patty jumped in her cage, though tense before the change in the pair was more prevalent to her prey instincts. It wouldn't be easy, but Jade told Rosalina to get closer for a smell while trying to picture the muscle group attached to those canines draw back in. It was difficult when hungry, but more so when you are a new vampire; that was a truth Jade never forgot. Watching closely, Jade prepares to step in at any moment.

Patty's eyes darted wildly, searching her cage for some escape for some time before it was clear to Jade that Rosalina was not able to perform the task given to her. The metal cage tapped against the table audibly affirming the fear visible inside. Tufts of hair stood ready to spit out something in an attempt to deter or defend itself.

Frustration creased Rosalina's brow as she faced the unfamiliar challenge. In order to calm herself it would help to close her eyes, but Jade knew just how unable to do that Rosalina might feel. Giving up, Rosalina flicked her eyes up, looking for some help. Jade understands the confusion on the concept but talks her through relaxing her body.

"Breathe in and feel the relaxation begin to roll over you. We need the opposite of aggression and tension to retract the fangs." The base of elongated teeth wasn't any wider than the average canine; it came to be extended and went back to appear normal. "Doesn't hurt at all, but picture something that makes you feel comfortable and happy."

At this, Rosalina closed her eyes and inhaled like she was told and pictured something to make her smile beam. From what Jade knew, maybe it was a large bakery shop the woman had said she wanted. There was a gasp of surprise as Jade watched the fangs slide back for

Rosalina. Rosalina grinned slightly as she asked to try again. Letting her proves to be the trick not only to keeping the cheerful smile going but also to getting the gist of the process figured out as she repeated her actions. "Now I'm going to take her out and show you just slightly what to do."

Jade took Patty out, holding the rabbit as firmly as usual. When fangs came out, hungry or not, the animals were uncomfortable and often kicked about. When Jade started feeding off animals, it took her a few tries to figure out their veins and arteries. It wasn't like a human; they were familiar, and almost everyone subconsciously knew them like the back of their hand.

Rosalina winced and groaned at the same time. Of course, despite her new desire, she was not used to seeing someone bite through rabbits' fur for blood. Rosalina resisted the urge to breathe while watching until Jade sealed the bite so Patty would not lose too much blood in the time it took to show the steps. Closing the wound smudges the usually white coat in red, driving more responses from Rosalina.

"You want to try?" Jade asks but gets a head shake from Rosalina. A moment later, though, Rosalina nods instead.

"I don't want to... Can you stop me?" It is Jade's turn to shake her head.

"If I try, many things could happen, mostly Patty would end up more than a little hurt. If you want more control, prepare for the moment you taste blood and think of something sad or emotional; hopefully, it will distract you into having some sense to release. I will say if it doesn't, Patty is my oldest animal. That's not helpful, but it is meant to be a good thing."

"Okay. It doesn't really make me feel better, just so you know." Rosalina let her teeth extend once more while Jade kept Patty still until Rosalina had her own hands on her and realized she wasn't that difficult to hold. She looked at the reddened coat and centered her mouth above it. Rosalina struck precisely where Jade had placed her teeth minutes ago. She hit the mark, yet Patty struggled only slightly due to the paralyzing agent in Jade's bite; a small tear caused more blood to spill. Whatever Rosalina might be thinking about, it wasn't as distracting as Jade had hoped. At the sound of Patty yelping in her own squeaky way, Rosalina pulled back and practically thrust her back into Jade's arms.

"I got distracted thinking about if there was something in the bite to calm them down." Rosalina says, feeling ashamed that she lost focus.

Nodding understandingly, Jade quickly closed the wound and bobbed her head in a gesture for Rosalina to follow her to the kitchen. Rosalina followed, holding a hand to her mouth as if trying to avoid making more of a mess.

"We do paralyze when we bite. It's a bit surprising that Patty did anything. I didn't feed from her, but my bite left something in her." Jade answered Rosalina, seeming to ponder the question, too. "I suppose that your venom hasn't piled up. It worked on your first use, but maybe not on her. Interesting..." They bathed Patty gently, followed by pets and treats; this time around, getting the calm rabbit from before took much longer to come back. Since she's older, Jade wouldn't use her again for a while to let her forget about the ordeal. Patty was weak, and until Rosalina could learn to feed properly, they couldn't use up the animals she had here. This didn't escape Jade as they finished up in the kitchen, and Jade led them to where she kept the animals.

Once down the cellar stairs, Jade saw the impressed look on Rosalina's face. The room looked designed for the animals but functional for everything else someone might want to do down there. Laundry, resting on the couch, TV, music, and even a small storage space.

"How did you manage to get this? Did you hypnotize someone?" Rosalina asked, not seriously asking the latter of the questions even though she honestly couldn't be too sure what vampires could or couldn't do. She'd seen strength, her senses were heightened, and fangs; for such a fantasy life come true, she didn't ever think it to be so natural.

"No, I have been around long enough to pay as much as needed to get this place. I scoped it out and knew I needed it. Not to say some power of persuasion isn't possible for us."

"How long?"

"I was born in fourteen-o-two. Nearly six hundred and three years since I was changed."

"Wow, so you were twenty weird, though I guess me being twenty-two might be a sore topic."

"Really, I mistook you for younger." It wasn't that not being over twenty bothered Jade. It just was one of those things you know doesn't fit who you are. "Young but wise." She adds, remembering the way Rosalina spoke at the diner.

"Why would you move here of all places? You must have been everywhere by now." Jade hums but doesn't answer before retreating up the steps. Following her intrigued now, Rosalina exclaims. "Oh, come on, tell me, please. I've lived in New York all my life, one place or another, why not France, Spain, or Italy?" She stopped at the top of the steps upon seeing Jade's face once she reentered the kitchen. Jade stared off coldly before facing her. Having uttered the question in the first place, Rosalina felt if the daggers in Jade's eyes were aimed at her, she might have died.

"No Italy." She sits, and Rosalina follows suit. "I hate to explain all of why, but I was changed in Florence and left there as soon as I could. My maker wouldn't hesitate to get one of his minions back. So, I stay away from Italy."

"Minions, that's what you were to him?"

"I have no intention of treating you the same way. Just because I felt I had no choice but to follow my makers' orders doesn't mean you have to follow mine. I fumbled with what I could do and what I should do far longer than you will anyways." Whatever Rosalina wanted to ask next stopped as Jade said this. Jade used her hesitation to change the topic once again. "I was thinking we might want to spend this next two weeks out. Somewhere we can practice and not necessarily get caught."

"Fine, I can leave it." Rosalina says dropping it with a smile. "Where'd you have in mind?"

"Mohonk Preserve into High Falls. Let's see... We have a few hours. I'll pack, but you should rest up in the room. If it's not normally busy, we can stop by your place once the sun goes down."

"No, I live in a small apartment building." Rosalina says letting Jade lead the way back to the small museum-like room. More aware, she looks over the most unique pieces as Jade rummages through her closet before handing her a fresh set of clothes.

"You need to throw those that you are wearing away. Shower, rest if you can, and we will probably leave in a few hours." There's a hint of urgency in Jade's voice. Perhaps all the talking mixed with the mess she'd caused with the homeless man Jade needed a few minutes to process. Rosalina realized she, too, needed some time. She was feeling a little overwhelmed and worried.

A warm shower was just the thing Rosalina needed to feel the chaos and tension dissipate. Wrapped in a towel, she walked the room. Awed by the tricorn that could've been a pirate's sitting next to the cutlass the way it was. At the sight of an armband, a phantom chill ran through her; it looked as old as WW2, barring a six-sided star on it, meaning it was very much from that painful time long ago. These were just a few of the oddities in the room behind glass on shelves or in cabinets, though she wouldn't pry any further.

She dresses in the comfortable, clean clothes Jade gave her: a blue tank top with a high rising neckline and lace lining that gave it a gothic look. Not only did she and Jade seem to wear the same size they had the same taste even if Jade's might be a lot more refined than hers. Landing on the bed as she slipped on the black jeans, Rosalina realizes just how comfortable it felt. It had to be, she supposed; if resting but not sleeping was ever uncomfortable, what would be the point in laying down?

It was for the better that she decided to lie down as she was now imagining some of the past Jade was running from. The possessions filling the room seemed to reveal how on edge or notorious for not sticking around one place too long Jade was. Though this was evident, Rosalina could also see past that and catch a glimpse of the woman who would help someone and choose to stay here of all places for some reason. The desire to find somewhere to belong despite her heart and head being on different sides of the fence.

The more the blonde lay with her eyes closed, the more the silence shattered into loud blips of scattered sounds. A picture would form in her head as a snagging zipper rippled closed or soft padding crossed the wood flooring of the house. Her nose added to the image beyond the room of what she dubbed artifacts. The picture forming began to change as she realized what each sound or smell was for.

Metal heating the plastic zipper as its snagged spot is gone over and over until it closes. Jade's darker hair wisps under the AC, leaving a lingering scent of jasmine from shampoo. She heard the distinct tapping of nails on a hard surface sometime later. While one hand was busy on a table, the other seemed to be stress-picking at fabric; the sound alone made Rosalina open her eyes, thinking that was such a bad habit.

Straightening up the bed before she left the room, she didn't need to have super hearing to know Jade wouldn't let her get down to the kitchen where she was to see her stressing. Sure enough, no nails were clicking or picking as she opened the door to the kitchen. Only the pouring of food into dispensers. This was how she planned to take care of the animals while she was gone.

"What about coming back to play with them or exercise?" Rosalina asked.

"They have outside locks on their door. I'll just have to leave them open a bit. They will get the gist of what to do. If it's cold or dark out, they more than likely will come back in. I'll check on them occasionally until we are done."

"Ok," Rosalina says, wanting to ask what was bothering her but also not wanting to intrude on something personal.

"Are you ready then?" Jade asks, looking softly at her. Perhaps realizing she was being colder.

"Yes. I'm nervous, but yes." Rosalina says as Jade walks down to the cellar with a container, Rosalina takes up the second. It was much larger than she could have lifted before without some effort, but now she was not even troubled with it. "Wow, I know I have used my strength already, but this is crazy."

"Well, you may have difficulty recalling what happened over time anyway. I did, at least." Jade took the second container from Rosalina and placed it in the fox's pen. It's wide and tall but fits perfectly. She seems always prepared when it comes to them.

"It was like a dream, more of a nightmare because I was disturbed by it until I was myself." Jade hums at first, like hearing this sounds familiar. Then she places a hand on Rosalina's to stop her from returning upstairs for a moment.

"It's not going to happen again if I can help it, so I take the blame for your first encounter with feeding being a messed-up nightmare." Rosalina smiles to convey how she believes Jade when she says this. Jade's hand leaves hers as she heads back up before her. Rosalina follows, wondering if the goosebumps were her instincts, then what were they trying to tell her now.

Climbing into the packed car, Rosalina's thoughts settled on how different Jade was acting from the first time they met when her heart pounded at Jade's smile. At least now she wasn't a complete mystery, though if her heart was still beating, she'd be so embarrassed while it thumped away because of how close they sat. The drive for Rosalina to collect her possessions was brief, but when it ended, she felt the tension was gone as soon as they pulled up to the building's front door. That tense feeling remained gone even though Jade suspiciously kept checking around during the drive.

4 |

Not a Vacation

In the dead of night, the pair trekked through known preservation hiking trails to set up camp in a cave behind a waterfall. Rosalina had never seen such beautiful trails and forests. In fact, she even wondered if she would be able to do much in a place like this. She knew Mohonk and High Falls were not the only preserves around, but could they practice the essential things in the two weeks Jade said they'd be able to?

Jade didn't seem fazed by her hesitation as she hammered their tent's stakes into the stone floor; no one was taking them out but them. After all, the longer-than-expected drive was pretty direct; these trails were closed, but they snuck in and were unquestionably where Jade intended to be. After finishing touches, the women still had time to practice, so Jade led the way to a clearing.

Surrounding them were trees in all directions now. The waterfall was far behind them, as was a larger but similar sound in front. Was she supposed to find her way back to camp? Rosalina wondered. She was sure it would be easy to do; after all, she'd kept track of which direction they started from and could hear the waterfall's differences in size based on the crashing waters. Rosalina stood ready not daring to underestimate Jade, even if she admitted to having never taught anyone before. As Rosalina's ponders there next actions her thoughts are interrupted when Jade's voice cuts through the sound of crashing water surrounding them.

"Let's get started. Near the other waterfall, you probably hear, is a group of tall trees. First, you should find your way to the waterfall, and second, we will start with your strength. Learning to control it is important for ensuring you aren't using too much or too little."

"You want me to climb trees?" They were definitely in the best place for that. "But isn't this a preservation? What if I break something?" Rosalina asked, her expression showing confusion.

"It will be easy at the start... if you don't knock it over trying to jump into one from running. After you get to a certain height, it won't be so easy since the branches could be strong or weak."

"Okay, so running and climbing. Should I know anything about running?"

"Just don't trip... it's more of a learn-by-doing sorta thing." Jade smiles and pulls her shoulders up into a shrug, very well knowing she is not being helpful. Still, she gives a notion to start whenever Rosalina is ready.

It's obvious the waterfall is ahead of them by the crashing Rosalina can hear, but now she wonders if this will not be as straightforward as she thought. It wasn't as if she couldn't just run through the maze of trees, but the more she focused on running and seeing, the less she could concentrate on the sound, so she ended up several miles further west than she was trying to go.

Upon finally reaching the waterfall, Rosalina marveled at its height, realizing it had to be the tallest in the entire area. The trees on top were big, but the group Jade had been talking about was clearly not far off to the other side that Rosalina came through. However solid and sturdy they looked, Rosalina remembered what

Jade said and took her time. For every branch that broke, a twinge of guilt filled her.

Jade watched her struggle from below where she piled up the branches that fell and seemed ready if Rosalina did too. Being high up and less able to grab anything, she began trying to climb like she did the wall with her fingers. However, it only caused the tree to splinter, with it not being as solid. Halfway to the height of the waterfall, she only had the size of an average tree left to go.

She looked at another tree, thinking it would be easier than the one she chose. As soon as she imagined jumping, she also could see it ending badly. She pulled herself up another inch by wrapping her arms around the trunk. This might have looked like an attempt by someone frightened of heights, but it seemed to get her to the next offshoot.

Carefully getting high enough to use her foot since the branch below appeared strong enough. Rosalina eagerly reached for the next one, achieving this small feat, only to find she was too short. Rosalina clung to what trunk was left at the near-top of the tree because she reckoned she couldn't safely get down now. Jade appeared to have far less trouble in the tree next to hers, sitting among the thinnest branches, resting with an arm around the trunk; Jade was beaming, probably using her strength to make it seem so easy.

"Great, honestly, not as much firewood as I thought we'd get." She called out. "I'd say jump down, but you'll hurt something. If not you, then probably the ground and roots."

"What do I do then?" Seemingly, Jade cared about this place but at least had concern for her first. Jade leaped over to Rosalina's tree in the blink of an eye, and there were barely any other signs of impact while it swayed.

"Trust me." Jade says taking a spot lower than Rosalina where the trunk was wide enough for both of them. She gestured for Rosalina to lower herself carefully. Once beside her, Jade adjusted their position so Rosalina could wrap her arms around her shoulders. Jade used one arm to support Rosalina's waist, keeping her close, and suggested she keep her legs tucked up as best as she could. "Here we go."

Like a roller coaster, they burst down, over, and around until they reached the ground. It all happened so fast, but Rosalina hadn't seen anything so smooth and elegant in all her life. Jade looked quite proud, noticing nothing had fallen in her wake. Her grin effectively slowing the way Rosalina lowered her feet to the ground and slid her arms from around Jade's neck. When she did, she shook the jasmine from her senses, took a stepped back, feeling more astonished at what they had done.

"I can't believe I did that without planning how I was going to get down." Rosalina groans.

"My way wasn't so bad, was it?" Jade asks innocently, making the blonde bite her lip as she still feels the excitement of speeding through the air, practically flying. The grace Jade kept with each bounce and the sureness was impressive.

Since dawn was nearly there, they left and returned to their cave and tent after Jade showed Rosalina the easier path. Of course, it was easier to go around the cluster of trees bridging Mohonk preserve, and high falls that Rosalina tried to rush through and instead cross over a trickling stream. Back at their camp, Jade brought more than enough for Rosalina to do while she typed. Supposing she took time off from work, Rosalina curiously wondered what she was writing.

The tent was big enough for ten people; in the area that was meant to be her bed, Rosalina sat "reading" a book. She hoped to see anything revealing about her maker. However, nothing stood out. Not the way she typed away or the way she perplexed over it. With a sigh, Rosalina closed her book and laid back, pondering how she'd get anything out of her maker.

"You can ask me, you know." At that, Rosalina jumped, surprised Jade had noticed her interest. "You were staring a bit too long at the book." She says as if reading her mind. "What are you concerned about?"

"I'm not concerned, well, aside from how I'm going to get where you are in two weeks. I was curious about what you are doing. Is it work-related? You don't give much away, so I couldn't tell if it's for fun or work."

"Oh, mostly for fun. I publish under a lot of fake names. In actuality, they are all fake names. I haven't used Jacopa Di Fazio since I died. Anyway, this isn't what I do for work. I build computers... Can't really do that here."

"But you can do that?"

"Yeah, hotspot, and I have a program that lets me work on my laptop at home and my tablet or phone when I am out. Plus, the solar generator helps." She points to the unit in the back, which Rosalina had already noted how well Jade had packed. The generator helped light up the tent since behind the waterfall was a bit dark. Not that Rosalina minded much after getting burnt when she tried peeking out past the waterfall; the sun faced the cave until mid-morning, after which it crossed over the trees from the east.

"You like writing that much?" Rosalina asks, wondering just how long she'd perfected this system too.

"I never could have when I was younger, not at that time, but I loved books. I had a duty to my family and the community. Now it's easy for me to pursue this, especially now that women can write openly too." The pair effortlessly slipped into a conversation about it, making the many daylight hours seem shorter.

The water fell with a loud enough crash to cover what little noises they made, but that didn't keep Rosalina from worrying about getting caught. Someone spotting the light in their camp or the generator charging outside had yet to occur by day three, helping Rosalina to worry less. Training exercises took place at night, which were unexpected lessons to Rosalina, given where they were. The results at the end of each day tremendously changed how they both felt about their time restrictions.

Especially with tablet games, board games, and books to distract them, Rosalina's doubt and worry turned to eagerness for more the next night. Jade, amid planning lessons, joined in casual conversations. Mostly she enjoyed watching Rosalina's enthusiasm when explaining several things Jade had yet to experience, such as games centered around old movies or shows. These games and many topics they spoke on were things Jade hadn't been into much of her life.

The world was constantly changing, and she was lucky she figured out the basics when electronic devices became a daily thing. A small thought of the future formed as a sudden realization hit Rosalina that they would see the coming changes over the next century. Jade saw the excitement on Rosalina's face as she kicked off the power and hotspot to save the other half for the next day.

"So next thin-" whatever Rosalina was about to say next froze on the tip of her tongue.

"I think I can get a great picture from up here." Said a voice from somewhere beside the waterfall. Someone was climbing the rocks.

"Josh, be careful."

"It's fin- whoah!" They could hear the audible crumble of stones as his footing slipped. He must have reached the top because where he fell was straight into the water. He had dropped well before his companion could even make a sound. There was a splash, thud, and crack.

"Ah!" Came a strangled cry and more splashing as the one called Josh sat up, clutching his head, and his companion rushed to help. Silhouettes of the pair could be seen struggling in the depths of the basin. Josh removed his hand from his head, pushed up, stumbled, and placed his hand back on his head. He was unsuccessful on his own due to being drenched in water or concussed, but with help, they made progress. The companion greatly supports the one named Josh.

Before Rosalina could tell blood was quickly clouding the water, Jade had her mouth muffled by a cloth and arms bound to her torso in a silver-lined rope. Searing pain came from the binding across her arms. Rosalina's eyebrows pinched, not thinking so much about how nothing was burning around her chest due to the clothes and more about the speed at which Jade reacted. However, the pain and Jade's speed were losing their surprise as her focus narrowed on her increasing desire. Not a muscle could be moved even though Rosalina struggled and began to growl into the cloth filling her mouth.

"Shh," Jade whispered into the frantic blonde's ear, hugging her from behind with a gentleness the situation did not likely need. As much as Jade's closeness bridged her conscience with her overriding instinct, Rosalina still wanted to reach the source of the blood despite the companion having dragged the man to the path again and tried calling for help. Josh fussed he was alright, but from inside the cave, the blood that could be seen said otherwise.

With no Wi-Fi to get help, the worried friend dragged the other back to someone who could help. Remarkably, it hadn't taken too long for them to find someone and for a team to patch him up enough and hurry him to a hospital. Jade unstuffed Rosalina's mouth when human ears couldn't hear her growling. The animals would scatter for the night, but at least her newborn wouldn't regret killing another person or, worst case, two.

"I'm sure you are in pain, but it's for the best," Jade said, aware Rosalina wouldn't answer her. "I didn't want you to know I brought that... but I wanted to be prepared for something like this." Inspecting her raw hand, Jade sits at the entrance of the cave.

The commotion had dissipated by nightfall, and the blood had long since drained downstream. Rosalina's senses were clear enough once more, to express her needs and wants. She needed to feed but wanted to feed on animals, not humans. Taking her at her word, Jade carefully un-binds her, only taking a few extra moments to wear some gloves this time.

"It's likely all the animals will be challenging to find tonight. Let's get some training out of this. Any slight noise after today's atmosphere, your prey will flee. If they hear you, you have to let them be. Try and try again until you get one by surprise. No killing, either. Learn the control you need to, as it will be hardest at times like now. I'll be watching out, but this is all you." Jade says encouraging her to give it her best try.

Without hesitation, Jade disappeared, leaving Rosalina to her training. Still feeling the stinging from where the silver embedded into her skin all day, the need weighed on Rosalina's mind; she forced herself to follow the rules. A handful of times, an animal heard her, she would huff in frustration and start over. Listen, track, then sneak until finally, she caught a deer.

Despite sensing eyes on her, Jade let Rosalina settle her hunger for herself. Maybe that trust to have a good enough heart to stop partly kept her from falling into the darkened tunnel that feeding begged her to enter. Jade's presence filled Rosalina with comfort, much like when Jade wrapped her arms around her in the cave or used her nickname. The surprising part of her ability to relinquish the deer came when she realized the power she still had to stop whenever; that support was there, but she did not need it.

After the deer staggered off, Rosalina turned away to find Jade no longer hiding but proudly standing behind her. A breeze swept by, whipping the blonde's hair into her eyes. She couldn't help but be amazed at the gaze in Jade's eyes once she fixed it back to one side. She was transfixed on Rosalina with a smile that said she'd missed her.

"You okay?"

"Mrs. Gardiner." She whispered the name, and Rosalina was nearly speechless.

"My great granny? What about her." Just like that, Jade's expression snaps back to normal.

"You always smelled like coffee, but I guess with the shower, rain, and all the training, you just smell like a lady I knew. She and her husband. It's probably someone else, not your great...great granny." She denies any relation despite every word she says, making Rosalina believe somehow it is true. Once back at the cave, Rosalina flops across her side of the tent, layered in blankets.

"What a vacation this has turned out to be." Sitting up cross-legged when Jade says.

"It's not a vacation."

"I know, but my job thinks it is." Rosalina gets nothing back. "Okay, so how do you know Mrs. Gardiner then if it's not my great gran."

"Well, in the late stages of the war, 1938, I was in New York then. There was fighting in the streets, some buildings were on fire, and this couple was trapped. It took all my strength, and I was badly burned, but I healed in front of them before I could hide it. Grateful and not disturbed, they offered me their home as repayment. I was off on my own at the time. I helped them repair their shop too for their kindness."

"My great-grandmother Jacqueline told me that story when I was 6. I remembered it so much that everyone insisted it wasn't real. She was 90, so they said she was just spinning tales. That story is what made me love supernatural things."

"Damn." Jade rubs her fingers down her face and up through her hair. "Fine, it was your relative. I guess I didn't want this to be weird."

"I think it's a fascinating example of how a chain of events can impact the future."

"I just passed Hell's Kitchen one day, and the way her fragrance was there made me think it was the city like it was calling me to stay. Then I realized it was you, and I knew there had to be a connection, but I tried to avoid crossing that line. I knew it wasn't just the smell when I met you in person. It was something about you."

"Cross that line? Like what mingle with humans?"

"I already have done that."

"Right. Probably wasn't your first time in the coffee shop. Then what do you mean?" Silence followed as if that was answer enough. Strangely, Jade looked all but heartbroken while Rosalina thought about it. "Oh. Oh! You mean I've been biting my tongue thinking that was some maker newborn thing."

"Hardly, me and my maker never! Bwahaha!" At the thought of it, the laugh pushed past Jade's restraint to escape. Rosalina felt her blood stir at hearing Jade's laughter for the first time. "You have been far more fascinating than anyone else I've met. Others I liked but never drawn to. It feels awful being your maker, knowing how I feel."

"It's not weird. Well, it's not weird to me. I've liked women for a while. Six hundred years, and you never liked women?"

"I have. I guess it's not weird..."

"Nope! Now... what are we gonna do if something happens again? I really don't like your rope." Rosalina asks, offering a reprieve to Jade.

"Uh, we'll deal with it, but we can practice fighting a little tomorrow. You can't have someone get one over on you so easy."

"You sure you'll be able to handle me if I go berserk."

"Definitely. Don't worry."

The events of the previous day and the tension through the night were not exhausting but made anything else seem unnecessary as they waited out the coming day. Without any interest in the distractions surrounding them, the feeling they had both been ignoring was building with anticipation. How deep did the interest they each knew the other felt go? Neither felt sure enough to talk, so they sat in silence.

There was no warmth to feel, any heart pounding to hear, but there was something electric bouncing between them in the cave. Jade itched to reach over. Take up Rosalina's hands wrapped around a pillow and kiss the knuckles to feel the energy spark. Yet as daylight slipped away, she pulled off her covers to sit up, still unable to express her own level of interest to Rosalina.

Watching Rosalina gently roll herself into a sitting position and leave the pillow with a glum look, Jade realizes the one thing she can do. She'd been training her this whole time; instead of remembering, she just gave up humanity. She needed a reminder of how things can still be fun.

What with all the stress, a more uncomplicated night might be nice. An easy night meant they could check on the animals and give them a night in. Jade faced Rosalina's determination with renewed excitement; she would give her the thrill every vampire enjoys. The run, the feeling of speeding through cities in minutes.

Rosalina was buried in learning how to feed, when to feed, and how to stop feeding. The strength, hiding, and chase training were as necessary as food but more to prevent discovery for keeping appearances. If they focused on the worst feature of a vampire, would she really want to be one?

"Why are you looking at me like that?" Rosalina asks, not seeing what she'd done to earn such a look.

"Tonight, we are going back to the city."

"For good? I didn't think I was ready should I get the car." They had parked it safely out of sight.

"No, we are just checking on the animals."

"No car?"

"No car, just follow me and keep up. I watched you run before, and it was alright for the first time and where we are. Don't be afraid to use more power this time. Just push off from your toes and let your foot land on its own after each step." Jade demonstrates this at first and then heads off towards Hell's Kitchen at a jog brought to a high sprint. When Rosalina catches up, she spots Jade dodging bushes and the few and far between lights, much better than any normal person, and quickly follows her lead. "Avoid lit areas, and it's gonna happen, but try to not be held up by debris or other such things in the air. Mouth closed is best, and here...wear these for your first long-distance run."

Rosalina took the eye protection Jade handed her, already having some dirt and dew spitting into her eyes. As they reached city roads, the lights danced in and out of her peripheral. Jade watched Rosalina control her footfall on the first rooftop they encountered, growing more impressed at how well she adapted, like briskly running across a balance beam perfectly.

Not one foot rested too long to make more than a light tapping sound or cause an imbalance. After an hour of running and carefully dodging openly lit areas, they made it to the townhouse cluster. The foxes and rabbits were curled up under their toy houses in the pens, with the door ajar still. Yes, the chill meant both pairs of animals had to huddle and utilize the tools in place to stay warm, but they were just as happy as when they left.

"Little guys did well, didn't you." She says, scooping out each soiled half of the rabbit's pens. "I forgot about this good thing we came back."

"They seem pretty good considering the chill in here."

"Thicker coats now though. I'll have to brush them out when we finish our training." Jade plucks a few loose fluffs of hair before leaving the two alone. The pair sat comfortably in the living room, Rosalina not feeling drawn to the outside distractions and Jade feeling like a great teacher after watching Rosalina succeed so well in the running all the way back.

Out of curiosity, Rosalina asked how Jade thought she was doing; even though Jade had no idea in comparison to another new vampire, she proudly said great. No one could understand a vampire like a vampire; with how Rosalina was picking her lessons up, Jade expected there would be questions to come that needed explaining. In her own experience, nothing was expected. No training, no fire, and no excitement

If her maker hadn't shut her down time after time and forced her through killing her dreams of returning home, she might have had this much excitement in her lessons once. The day he killed her parents to keep her with him, she strove to leave, but that wasn't out of passion anymore; it was anger. That wasn't this. Jade let the past slide away while she decided the best way to explain what Rosalina was asking.

"While we clearly exist and have control of our motor skills, our body has many things it no longer needs to focus on. Breathing, pain, or warming organs. Therefore, we can still function but do more. You adjust faster, and your mind can learn and process faster without all the other million signals garbling it all up."

"That's so amazing, so you can teach me self-defense much easier than I could have learned when I was mortal." Rosalina chirps excitedly as if oblivious to the bustle of the city outside. It was only thanks to the thick walls and windows surrounding them. The artificial lighting was just as obstructive to seeing what sat behind the curtains, and the more that time passed, the more it didn't matter as long as it worked to keep the outside world just that.

"Eager to keep up the training?" Jade asks, deeming the interest enough to maybe consider practicing carefully.

"Maybe to finish so we can focus on something else. Like a date."

"A-"Jade's mouth froze; what from is a mystery, and she choked out a reply. "Date? You want to finish training to have a date with me?"

"Of course, I know it's not something either of us is familiar with, but you said it before, and I agree, something about you draws me to you. I didn't believe I could run here today, but your smile and your enthusiasm locked me in. Now look, I'm in your house, and we didn't end up burning halfway here because I was taking too long to learn and struggling. I was just in the moment."

As soon as the words spilled out, Rosalina had no idea what to do but stop and at least try to keep herself from fidgeting full of nerves. She didn't want to take it back, but she knew it was incredibly early to ask for a date. People do it all the time, take someone's number and have first dates with strangers. They were going on two weeks into getting to know each other.

"I'd love to. There are a million places to take a date, but I think we can find a place." Grinning, Jade says this flirtatiously before transitioning the topic, however, by having Rosalina stand at one end of the sofa. Dragging the couch over and out of the way creates ample space for an easy, hand-to-hand fight. Some training would make the next seven hours fly by. "I've already given you a sad takedown. How about you get one free chance to get me back."

Responding to Jade's taunting tone, Rosalina steps forward. She studies her before choosing to fake left and try to seamlessly shoulder-check Jade in the waist. However, Jade sees the adjustments and pushes her downward, successfully sliding her through her legs in one motion. Turning around, Jade finds the stunned blonde is back on her feet.

"That was alright, but you'll have to do better."

"I really thought I'd get you if I faked a direction."

"I'm ancient, but I wasn't absent when people came up with that stunt." Rarely in the last several decades was laughter something of a common occurrence for Jade. Still, once more, the rarity that it became as natural as breathing once was.

During the time they practiced, time sped up. The sun was no longer lighting the crack above the curtains but brimming the bottom. Jade was confident Rosalina would settle this soon enough. Estimating that with all the slight advantages she'd managed this time, Rosalina would wipe the floor with her.

However much Jade saw coming, her couch did not. By the time the flurry of movement between them froze due to simultaneously locking arms, Jade hadn't expected Rosalina to pull off an old-school martial art maneuver after twisting them closer to the couch. Rosalina caught her footing and finished their round by rolling Jade over the back of the sofa.

The wooden frame cracked as Jade slid to the floor, speechless. While surprised at the follow-through, Rosalina quickly rights herself up from the cushion to help Jade climb to her feet. Waving her off, she sat there and motioned for Rosalina to join her. Jade's lips formed into a soft yet proud grin.

"I don't even know where that came from." Despite the pride glimmering at her, Rosalina hardly felt deserving.

"I bet you don't. You wondered if you could get me if you did something like that, so your instincts and body did it. Sure, you might have seen it before, but you improvised perfectly."

"Really? I thought I was using too much strength. I mean, I ruined your couch." The truth was around the legs of the furniture, the floor was cracked, but there was no sign that either of them noticed as they sat there falling into each other's gazes.

Licking her full lips, Rosalina leans in with a tilted head. Moments later, she claimed Jade's lips with a quick testing peck. The tight resistance in Jade's muscles melted away instantly like there was no need to have distanced herself all this time. A brush of their foreheads magnetized them together, causing Jade to exhale softly.

Returning the kiss, Jade felt fire and power surge, and then she felt the hair on her neck raise while a sound reached her ears. A faint tug came from Jade's hand for Rosalina to wait as they almost deepened their exchange. Before words could escape her mouth, though, Jade pressed one finger to her lips. Her eyes flickered around without moving her head, telling Rosalina something was up.

"We should go upstairs, right?" She suggests offering some form of assistance to the alarming situation. She listens for anything outside the house with her own ears but doesn't know what to listen for. This wasn't animals in the woods by any means.

"You go up. I'll lock up down here. I'll be just a minute." Slowly, they separated; Rosalina headed up while Jade remained sitting silently, assessing more than just the damage under the legs of the sofa. The slightest shift in pressure made a rubber sole squeak once more, pinpointing the whereabouts of a culprit just outside, observing from the rooftops. A flash of fury in her eyes speaks for her, but she is gone in moments with no one there to see her plans play out.

5

The Basin

When it only took an instant for the onlooker to be surprised and taken out with a swift snap of the neck, Jade knew she had not been dealing with her maker. Until she saw the observer's common face turning to cinders inside a furnace, the reality her maker's presence might've eluded her was worrying. Sure, the few blocks she had to carry the goons' body was not an easy solution, but it was a better one than how she disposed of the homeless victim the first night Rosalina was changed.

With the reminder of Rosalina waiting for her return, she began looking around to find the abandoned workshop still all clear to leave, and she vanished once more. From outside and above the streets, the stench of burning bodies was not as foul as a normal human was. However, it was something Jade would not like to linger around too long. There was a sense of urgency to get out of the city again in every stride back to her home.

Unlike Jade expected, Rosalina wasn't just sitting idly by. She had prepared the door to the fox's pen and was ready to leave again as soon as Jade was. There was much to discuss, but Jade couldn't bring up the kiss or anything else until they were a safe distance from more peering eyes. Rosalina accepted this without needing to be told, but Jade knew her persistence to know would return soon enough, so they took off in the night, not much later.

There was rain in the air as they started. When they made it to camp, they shook off practically all the water they had collected. Not only did the rain help their scent become drowned out, but it made a glimmer of light falling over soaked hair and skin very distracting. The pair sat at the waterfall cliff, watching every direction but not in silence as Jade normally would prefer.

"We had someone your maker sent watching us?" Rosalina asked, prompted by Jade's remark that started the conversation. The un-asked question, though, was how she knew it wasn't just a stranger vampire.

"Yes. I know he wasn't just some vampire watching us; we don't typically watch each other. We have stalker types that hunt humans but not other vampires. Besides, he wasn't here long, so he smelled like my old coven. You'll see you never forget a smell."

"Well, you didn't forget my great-grandmother and her husband, so I don't think I'll deny that."

"What do you feel like doing if he sends more? You might be all right next week; steer clear of tough situations and my place for a little while if you need to leave. There is no guarantee that that guy was alone until tomorrow night, but after you can decide." There wasn't a need to say all of this, but Jade heard herself rambling any-way. Rosalina wasn't frightened, though. Not by the idea of some old vampire barely trying to hold power over her maker. She was worried Jade would leave to protect her. Either return home to him or further away.

"I've already sacrificed everyone in my life to be myself. I have no one I need to reach out to anyone anytime soon." Rosalina was subtly saying she would follow her if needed. Clasping Jade's hand felt even more clarifying as they sat observing all the shadows that rested. Eventually, when none of the ones that did move were found to be anything more than the wind swishing tree branches around, so they retreated to the cave and awaited the next night.

Over the next two nights, they briefly surveyed and trained. The trip to town meant to ease Rosalina into experiencing the joys of their abilities, felt like ages ago. The kiss, the request for a date, and the urge to feel the connection left Jade ready to breath and try again. It was time to give Rosalina a date. Knowing the perfect spot, she invited Rosalina to follow her.

Stepping out past the curtain of water, a different night light greeted them. A crimson glow filled the forest and brimmed the treetops with dark ominous colors. It was a quick trip to the far side of the preserve, where the taller waterfall was. Once they reached the edges of the plunge pool, the moon cast its shade over the waters from above.

Anything but wonder and delight was impossible for either of them. Knowing the beauty that lay beneath the surface, Jade slips off her shirt and pants. Not dressed for swimming, but her under garments would do. Looking back at Rosalina, Jade waves her in.

Her silhouette melts into the water, leaving Rosalina to watch, anticipating her to resurface soon. Doubt worried Rosalina's face briefly before a trickle of excitement raced down her spine, as if the thrill of diving into potentially freezing water to get her maker to face her was more enticing than the fight training that still needed doing. She wouldn't deny it. As she dove in, feeling the water rush the length of her body, leaving no traces of cold sensations, she riddles how they'll make excuses to bundle up later.

Suddenly, all other thoughts failed as the depth revealed it was covered in life. It could take every second of breath for several hours to enjoy each bit of it. The longer Rosalina swam, she realized not even that would interrupt the wonder. Taking in the mild fish, the swishing seaweeds, and the thriving coral reefs, Rosalina glimpsed over anything else. When she finally caught sight of Jade's pure, amber-colored eyes lined with a golden shine further back, she kept going.

There were more wonders than could be counted. More untarnished colors to take in. Beyond the sights and the silk-like sensation of water gliding over the surface of Rosalina's skin, Jade swims upward, she follows. The water that could be frozen over in a month or so barely crackles as she breaks through the thin layer. It was a wonder, with the power of the falls, that it could freeze at all.

Blinking away the glinting drops of water across her lashes, Rosalina sought out her maker's eyes once again. As she rotated, two hands held her: one on her waist and another on her cheek. Jade's delicate palm rested on her cheek while her thumb strummed the damp, pale skin. Under the glaring red moon, the skin looked nearly natural.

As they waded closer to the waterfall, Jade pointed out a ridge behind it they could sit on. Even with room enough to lie down, they pressed their backs to the wall and sat, resting their heads together. Jade tells more tales of Jacqueline and Benjamin and how she'd grown to know Rosalina's great-grandparents so well, being there to see them start the bakery and for everything up until Jade began standing out.

The ideal night might have been to give Rosalina a date in public to show her that normal life wasn't gone, but this pleasant chatter and moonlight seemed to have the same effect. Across Jade's legs, swirls a finger as Rosalina listens. While the temperature was not causing the skin to bump up, the touch made it feel like it was. A form of a giggle escapes. Placing her hand over her partner's hand Jade stills the action.

"Stop dear, it's distracting." Rosalina smiles, a little amused at such a notion. Rosalina pecked Jade's cheek and flipped her hands playfully.

"Sorry, continue!" She urged.

"I don't know; it's getting to be quite early." Jade teasingly makes to move as if to leave. In an attempt to pull her back, Rosalina ends up slipping suddenly into the water. She resurfaced to find Jade bracing herself on the ledge, bursting with laughter. There wasn't a human soul for miles as the melody rang out. The trees seemed to shiver at the silence that followed. Every minor detail stood out to Rosalina as she bobbed in the water: the subtle stick of damp skin as Jade let her cheek rest against the stone facing her, the alternating sounds of nocturnal owl settling down, and the chattering of rousing animals like moms coaxing their little ones awake.

The sun had not yet begun to rise, the dawning hour was nearing. As Rosalina heard the stirring animals, the trickling sound of water swallowing Jade's foot then legs never reached her until the sweeping flow across her waist surprised her. Adjusting to see beneath the surface, a hand waited held out asking to be taken. Suggesting a swim together before returning to the cave.

In paler moonlight, the basin revealed far more than the red did before. Even as they trained rigorously over the next few days the memory of the moons sinful color lingered in Rosalina's mind. They worked on everything from fights to escapes all while focusing on self-preservation, "survival instinct," Jade called it. The ultimate subconscious defense for the immortal. What felt like uncontrollable moments where her feet would move even just two steps in one direction, thrusting her from a fatal blow. Rosalina could see the need to train to learn, so it was less of a wild card. Training would turn it into a five-steps ahead kind of skill.

To feed was a new second nature as was healing and heightened senses. Along with these, many skills could be honed to be as latent as possible. Years of practice would offer more, but to know from nearly the beginning what your limits where and how to get better would mean better chances out there on her own. Jade insisted in case anything ever happened to her. Rosalina knew she shouldn't feel the sting thinking about that reality, but she did despite knowing her for only a short while. Even though Jade got distracted listening deep into the forest at times, she seemed obviously concerned about protecting her. Either as her maker or out of affection, Rosalina, wasn't sure which was Jade's motivation.

A few nights after their visit to the waterfall, Rosalina found herself longing to return, if only to see the real Jade—the one who kissed her in the apartment and leaned into her touch. Nothing quite as longing and desirable stirred more than glances and meaningful touches. Reminding herself that this wasn't just a leisure trip, she didn't ask to go back or let herself take more than she was given. If they were to be connected forever, they would have that long to further these feelings. As these thoughts crossed her mind, Jade packed up her laptop, the books, and the mini solar generator. They were heading back after tonight; it was over already, and Jade was telling her that she felt confident that her resolve was stronger than the urges.

"As long as I keep up with feeding?" Rosalina asked, feeling that that was the key part. They hadn't discussed any of the city lifestyles effect on the training much. Out here, she was fine feeding and not getting caught, but to come all this way every night, it just wasn't reasonable if she needed something soon. "I won't be feeding as much in the city because there is less to exert myself with. I'll have to adjust still what if I mess up and find myself with a strong urge?"

Jade zips the bag closed and looks at her with a blank expression, which softened into a gentle smile.

"You can come over...I'll always be there to help you." Her eyes said she meant it, giving Rosalina a slight comfort in this. When they stepped beyond the curtain of water, they walked differently, not to a destination but with a slow pace. They just talked. Since it was much later than just after sundown, the black night swallowed everything.

"I thought with the goons showing up, you would want to leave. You and I will have this connection regardless." Calling them that was almost less frightening than what Rosalina pictured them to be. Monsters, immortal mafia, or enslaved people.

"I've never felt so natural around someone, and distance is nothing between vampires." Rosalina says faintly a delicate whist fullness in her tone paints a picture for Jade.

"True, but I haven't been bothered by them in a long time I have hopes it's going to end without trouble. All I've ever wanted was to live a simple life since I was changed." Jade pauses as she deeply expresses her current intentions to Rosalina hoping to relieve any concerns.

"Doesn't seem simple from all the things you've collected; they tell a very big story." Without needing to see it, Rosalina knew Jade felt panicked by this remark. "You don't have to tell me, of course. It's much different than asking why you moved to Hell's Kitchen." Visibly strained now, Rosalina tried to think of something else to bring up.

"I don't mind telling you long stories or not; it is my past, and you have to know all of me if I want to know all of you." The strain that sat there a moment ago has vanished. Now, at a creek not far from the larger waterfall, Jade steps one foot in and offers a lift to get Rosalina across. Jade guides her jump with her hands on her waist. To thank her, Rosalina took her hand and led her up to where she stood.

Foreheads nearly touching, Rosalina can see a recognizable glint in Jade's eyes. It reflected their first kiss. Had Jade not leaned in, Rosalina thought she might slip trying to keep herself up straight. Lacing their fingers just before closing the gap. As soon as they touched and swayed closer, there was a blissful feeling that once again Rosalina wondered if that was her feelings or Jade's. Swiftly as it came, a reeling wave of emotions shook her. Stumbling back a few steps, Jade looks stuck between rage and worry. Shaking from the pounding in her head, Rosalina loses her balance; despite trying to regain control, but forcibly crashes backward into a large tree.

The immense crack and squeaking sound echoed as the tree fell with a thud. Then, the full impact to the ground seemed to abruptly desensitize the overwhelming emotions. Amidst her descent, what attempts she made at staying standing must have caused her to swipe Jade's sleeve because it had three thin, fresh tears. Unaware of them, Jade quickly knelt on one knee to check Rosalina. For what, she wasn't sure.

"Is the pain gone?" Jade asks, her voice filled with concern. Rosalina nods, brushing debris from her pants. Leaves and bark shrapnel float in the dust in front of her hand, and she suddenly notices her nails have grown longer. Despite the startling realization, Rosalina tried not to get distracted. She looks up at Jade, confused and shaken by the ordeal.

"Either you have bipolar disorder, or that was something else entirely." The presence of any more waves of emotions is gone; still, Jade takes the joke at face value for what it is. A front in hopes of a proper answer. This time, Jade doesn't hesitate. She's not looking around but focused on her.

"I tried not to worry you. We had no interference, and then I felt his sick jealousy. Gabriel, my maker showed up not long after we left camp, I tried to remember that while we were talking, I even hoped he would leave us alone if I said that's all I wanted. Then we got closer, and I shouldn't have kissed you knowing someone was watching." Sincerely, Jade attempted to help Rosalina up, but when she pushed herself up and brushed off the rest of the dirt before being pressed for more with a glance that said, 'And then.' "I felt his anger and betrayal, and I became furious with him. The man who killed *my* parents to keep me in his grasp for a hundred years felt *betrayed*?! I've never had to tamper that in before."

"That was your feelings?" Not usually sifting through other people's feelings, so internally, Rosalina made a mental note of how the initial one's were dulled and the one's that followed were immensely Stronger. Enough to make her dizzy. "He's gone, gone where?"

"The city, probably my home. He's going to ruin anything I have. He may think this will have scared you away from me... I hope it hasn't." Rosalina leans with one hand against Jade's shoulder before removing her shoe, shaking bits out, putting it back on, and repeating with the other one.

"No. If anything, I hope Gabriel does think that, but he'll be surprised that it hasn't." She smiles. "I forgive you for the public display of affection. next time, let's be more on the same page." Just as true to everything her personality has been so far, they've faced it and moved on. The blonde was proving to be capable of handling far more on her plate than the average person. Even though they could have picked up the trail instantly to follow her maker, Jade pointed out they shouldn't leave anything this time in the cave. They de-stake the tent and pile anything camping supply related into the car. Anything of personal use, like the laptop and such, went into a backpack.

Only leaving behind what could be mistaken for anyone left behind camping equipment, they quickly took chase. Even if Jade listened for him, sirens and the nightlife would swallow any trace of him. They might not be able to stop him, but knowing how sure Jade felt that Gabriel was going to trash her home and flee back to his coven made their destination clear. Rosalina was comforted at the thought that if he didn't want to attack her out right in the woods, he wouldn't wait in the city to hurt her.

After what was probably the fastest trip back to the city, they arrived to find the neighborhood still in darkness. While no one was out right in the street, people surveyed from their home windows. Glass could be seen littering the sidewalk. The front door was wide open, the lights were still off, and silence greeted them as they quickly made their way inside. Far enough into the shadows that no onlookers could see them. Quietly Jade gestures she needs to look around.

While Jade starts where she can search for personal belongings, Rosalina moves to check on the animals for her, they were being awful quiet. When she entered the cellar, it was clear why. She should have sensed it. Smelt the drying spilled blood, heard the silenced heartbeats, but it still wasn't as second nature for herself as it was for Jade. Unable to fix their demise, Rosalina assumes Jade will know best what to do with them. Seeking her out, she moves through the kitchen while staying in the shadows, then heads upstairs, realizing that's where she'd gone.

At the doorway to Jade's room, the destruction is more prominent. Clearly, he knew where to hit her hardest. As if gently entering the room would make it easier, Rosalina remains silent as she approaches the side of the bed that Jade is rummaging under.

Floorboards were lifted out of the way, but what Jade was trying to get out seemed to be bigger than the hole at first. Once she got it, Jade stood up and held it close with a depressed sigh as she looked around the room.

"At least I still have this. Of all this history, this was the most important to me." A book that looked so old that the binding needed replacing. Its cover yellow, but that too even looked like time had changed it. Yet Rosalina could only see the book and Jade's expression through dazed eyes as she gripped the metal footboard of the bed. Taking in a deep breath and exhaling, she centers herself, hoping the sadness passes soon. Even as she thought this, the feeling began subsiding. Realizing her grip had bent the pole she removes her hand sheepishly. "Don't worry about it. I'm sorry I did it again."

"It's a lot to basically say goodbye to." Waving her concern off. "Are we sticking around to clean up?"

"Honestly... I can't do that; I can't keep you involved either. It's my mess to clean up, and I don't mean all this." Sirens were roaring nearer. It seemed someone had finally called the authorities.

"You want to face him alone? I won't just sit here, you know. I feel as involved as you are. He did all this to hurt you and frighten me. Fortunately, I don't scare easy, and you won't fall for that emotional taunting." Rosalina says refusing to remain in the city.

"I did before'" with no more time to spare, she packs the book carefully, and they slip out through the window onto the roof and leave as one cop car after another lines up on the street. Seemingly, this was fine; anything of importance to Jade was now in her backpack. Without any idea what Jade had planned she stays close. "we'll have to head to a friend's place in the Canadian mountains. He's closest and might have something to help give us an upper hand."

Being it was only one in the morning, they crossed the city by rooftops, making their strides match as to go nearly unnoticed. As they reach Canada, the snow is more present; even the base of the mountain is covered. When they paused at the base, Rosalina gazed in awe, never having been able to travel like this before. Walking a few paces into the undisturbed snowfall, she hears Jade finally exhale what must have been a steaming last few hours of tension in one breath.

"By the time we reach my friend's place, the sun will be up. If he's not following us now, he won't bother trying now." Jade says sound confident Gabriel was not following them.

"That's good. To be honest, I'm a little worried we might need more help with how menacing his actions were back at your home." She thought of the poor animals and how, even though Jade hadn't asked, it must have been just as sad for her. Rosalina knew she could see it in her eyes. "I'm sorry, too. They might not have been pets, but you had good honest kindness and intentions with them."

"Fuck... I hate I couldn't bury them." A sting of anger tapped over to Rosalina, but her own distaste of the fear-bidding maker's deeds matched it. Jade didn't seem to mind. Perhaps she had grown used to it from her own experience or maybe it didn't translate that way.

"It's not your fault. People might be perplexed about animals in pens, but it looked like an explosion or something. I doubt beyond us anyone will ever know what happened or what comes next." Rosalina says, offering scant comfort.

"Next, we meet Ward." More than happy to switch topics, Jade peaks Rosalina's interest once more in this friend of Jade's.

"What is he like?" she asks as they reach a level incline. They haven't got much in gear, but being rather early still, no one can see that.

"Ward? Oh, he's a true friend but a bit different." Jade says with a grin

"Different, how?" Even though it was going to go unanswered, Rosalina asked this in hopes of some sort of hint.

"You'll see." They picked up the pace into a run again. Each step felt strange to Rosalina. Using the speed they had yet still sinking inches deep on each stride. Eventually, the sensation falls into the background. After traversing up what had to be thousands of feet, a cougar runs up beside Jade as if to say hello. Running alongside them, elegant and of pure muscle, only to moments later spring off meeting up with others of its kind that appeared to be waiting near a cluster of trees. Glints of light reflecting off the falling flakes cast rainbows, but only from behind clouds is the rising sun able to caress the mountain's west side.

Winding to the east side, it seemed they were nearing their destination. Hundreds of yards away from a cottage tucked up against the surrounding mountain, Rosalina suspected it was intended that trees and snow made it somewhat less likely to be approached by anyone not intending to be there. Seeing that they were popping in unannounced so early, the pair made sure to stop this far from the home to assess if anyone was even up yet. With excitement to meet a friendly link to the long past that Jade undoubtedly has, Rosalina fidgets where she stands.

How did one so new to this life not wonder what next would surprise them? Would he be physically distinctive, or perhaps his temperament different? Was his past less heavy on his shoulders? Rosalina wondered if he had a choice. Did that make the change easier? Focusing her senses, she decides to listen for anyone stirring about inside the cottage instead of lingering on thoughts of what-ifs.

6

The Demon on the Mountain

Instantly, Jade and Rosalina picked up on two heartbeats. Calm and at rest with occasional paper scrapping as a page from a book turns over. Though still perplexed, three pages later, Rosalina follows Jade to the front door without rushing since the mountainside kept them protected from the sun.

"I wasn't expecting to hear a living person." Not sure what she meant to ask, Rosalina feels even more curious. "You made it seem like you had no other human friends."

"He's not human; anyone that does live up here refers to him as a demon. Like an old, cursed, and creepy cottage in a story."

"He's not really, just a lot of mystery about him. Like you, I take it?"

"Exactly." Without another word, Jade knocks on the door. When she jumps at the sound of a dog barking, Rosalina chuckles. A voice drowns out the dog, saying something to stop it. As the door swings open, Rosalina instantly glimpses the form of a tiny pup at the entrance. That is before she speechlessly observes how the man answering the door in the middle of a mountain is wearing an emerald-colored three-piece suit.

"Jade? I thought I wouldn't be seeing you so soon! Jinx misses you. Did you see her?" Without waiting for an answer, he faces Rosalina. Ungluing her gaze from his attire and meeting his eyes, she was greeted with a smile by the tall young-looking Serbian man; he stroked his chin as he looked her over. "You brought someone back with you. She looks simply sweet. Come in, I'm Ward, and this is Phantom."

"This is Rosalina. Since when do you have a puppy?" Leaning down, Jade lets him sniff her hand. She chose not to pet him until he bumped his nose against her finger. "Little risky having a dire wolf around, but he seems harmless."

At this remark, Rosalina looks Phantom over. His build does scream wolf, but she'd seen wolves that grew up kind. Typically, they grow attached to a caretaker, but nothing seemed to be injured or wrong with him. Questions about Ward and the wolf kept coming to mind, even with the urgent reason they came all this way. Jade made her way to some chairs around a small table. Despite a seat being available next to the one Ward's book rested on, Rosalina sat on the ground with Phantom, who curiously sniffed her out.

"I found him a while back and got him to trust me. He hasn't changed much, so I take it that's why he was alone." Phantom looks at Ward as if aware he was the subject of the topic. While Ward says this, the short puppy fur stands on end until he shakes his head. "So, what brings you back with another woman in tow?" The kind tone Ward greeted them with became serious, and his focus turned to the tale Jade was retelling of everything that had happened. Skimming over the more gruesome stuff about Rosalina's change and the personal time the pair spent together. Not against sharing, she filled in some things that Ward seemed intrigued by, how Jade trained her, and how she felt now that it was over.

"We covered much more than I expected when this whole thing started. I don't think I imagined the fiasco with her maker would happen. Now that it has, I expect it might be such a rollercoaster of drama if his actions speak for him." Rosalina says as it feels more like an open discussion again.

"Gabriele has always had an attachment to me. I never learned what it stems from love, psychotic, or what, but he's wronged me too much." Jade never explained everything, but she appeared to be ready to. "I was given the plague before I was changed. After, because I felt in debt to him for saving me, I was in his coven after I was changed. I wanted so badly to control myself enough to go home, but every day was challenging. So, I built up tolerance for ten years and tried to stay on his good side. More often than not, he was foul, but not to me. I just wanted to return to my family. He made it to my home before me the night I decided to leave, making sure to kill my mother and father."

Jade clung to the bag that was no longer on her back but in her lap as she said this. The material was so worn that Rosalina was sure that if Jade held the bag with her book any harder, it would burst into shreds. It must symbolize her love for her parents and the childhood she cherished. The following words slipped out of Rosalina's mouth.

"Why did you go back? You said you were with the coven for 100 years."

"I was.... I don't know if it was out of fear, depression, or if I felt trapped by his power over me. I watched him change others and learned he had many methods. One of them was having thralls give innocent orphaned children deadly viruses. It didn't sit well with me, given what happened to me, and I decided I needed to get free and far away from him. Whatever kept me, I eventually overcame it and left. Given time, I found my way thanks to Ward and some friends." Jade's grievous tone slips into a genuine one, like a promise for more than just one of these introductions. "I felt this emotional barrier we've had shift the night I changed her. All I did was cross my fingers, hoping it didn't mean anything. I should have called you at least."

"If only to get everyone together so we can kick his ass," Ward says, clenching a fist.

"As if just you and I can't handle him." Jade sets the bag down finally. "I offered Rosalina to stay behind, but she didn't want to have any of it."

"More so, I find it absolutely wrong that he doesn't even know me, let alone know or care who you are after all these years. I can't imagine what he gets away with but destroying your home, killing your animals, and making you flee a perfectly good home in the city. I could let you stand up for yourself alone. I'd feel so unsatisfied not having a hand in it." Phantom sprang up with a deep bark. One that called out like a rallying cry. His shape grew broader and taller than just a second ago. Looking at both Ward and Jade in shock she exclaims "wow I didn't know dire wolves did that!"

"They don't." Ward closes his book, forgetting to mark his spot. He was fully invested in this curious happening.

"Phantom, what is it?" Rosalina stands up as he faces her. He crosses to her and brushes her legs before facing Ward and Jade, sitting at her heel like a statue, a sign of a loyalty claim.

"I guess I just wasn't your type, huh, bud. Something of what you said did something to make him loyal to you. Wonder what is with the appearance change, though. You want to clue us in on that?" In response, Phantom paces a circle centered between the lot of them. With each step from one person to the next, his stance changes. Almost fierce and royal.

"He's an Alpha," Rosalina said; following that, he crouched low and growled at no one in particular. Assuming this demeanor caused his condition, Rosalina wondered out loud whom he had threatened. In an attempt to convey his story, the moment he growls, his form is forced back to a puppy once more. Clearly not getting it, Ward presses his hands together and opens them as a crystal ball appears between them. While Rosalina fumbles a term of surprise from her lips, he gently brings the ball downward to Phantom.

"Show me." Now that he understands the problem, he needs to know the cause. With a soft touch of Phantom's nose against the crystal ball, a picture swirled to life in it. As the alpha, his form was much larger than the others, but the pack looked hungry, starved even. They were filing in on a campsite. A burnt-out fire and darkness sat there, but then there were screams and growls. As the alpha Phantom did whatever it took to feed his pack, it was his job to corner the prey.

In this case, it was a small family, and only moments of silence passed between the screams and the sound of their hunger being sated. The pack of wolves leave the tent one by one, not just to be faced with a woman but a teary-eyed mother. None of them were hungry anymore nor felt threatened until her tears turned to fury, and she began muttering words. The other wolves back up behind the alpha while he stands his ground.

"I curse you to wear this shame." the woman yells, jabbing her hands at Phantom. Nothing seemed to happen for a moment, but then Phantom yelps. The others scatter while the woman takes hold of the wolf, becoming smaller and smaller by the scruff. "You might know of honor and loyalty, but this form you have will teach you justice and purpose. If it doesn't kill you like you have killed my family..." She tosses him aside before disappearing inside, where wails of her pain and loss close off the image in the ball.

"That's fucked up, blaming them for being hungry. They were on wild land." Ward looks pissed, and while he wishes he could have prevented this for that family and Phantom, he had no idea how to fix the curse. However, after the show and tell, Phantom sits beside Rosalina and barks as if to say something. While Jade and Ward might not sense it, Rosalina can, having always been good at reading people and animals.

"You want to help us?" another bark, and his proper form awakens again. "If you guys think it might help?" Rosalina asks, rubbing Phantom's head.

Both look stunned but agree because the four of them would make a formidable team. At the mention of a team, Jade exclaims she will need to plan and that whatever she comes up with needs to give them an upper hand over Gabriel. Ward offered some assistance in this, suggesting they follow him.

"Oh, by the way, I received a letter from the council. If you want to look, Jade, it's over in the cabinet." She looks slightly surprised but doesn't hesitate to pull out the folded paper he spoke of.

"Hmm. A rogue agent. That can't be good for them." Jade says, tucking it back into the cabinet before making her way over to them.

"I suppose it is just a notice to keep a lookout," Ward says, brushing it off like it wasn't something they would need to worry about with their intentions of leaving.

"What's the council for?" Having it brought up in front of her, Rosalina believed her curiosity would explode if she didn't ask. Ward stopped short of a chest, resting his hand on the lid as he turned to answer her.

"It's a supernatural council. A few folks formed it to help hide magic, creatures, and immortals from humans. It's a massive group that helps tremendously, even though it has changed over the last few hundred years. I joined to keep in the loop even though I'm out in the middle of nowhere." With that, Ward lifted the lid to take out a pair of studded earrings for each of them. Taking one of the pair, they have a feeling of something about them that Rosalina has no idea what it means. Not catching her confusion, Jade thanked him and immediately put them in her ears instead of a pair she was already wearing, so Rosalina followed suit. Still, the act of wearing them doesn't quite explain anything. It is only when Jade tells them that she will look up if there are any late flights for that night so they can be in Italy by early morning that Rosalina gets that they must have some power to reduce the sun's effects on vampires.

"of course, with you being new, you must be curious about them. Until you are even older than Jade, you'll have to have protection or items such as these." He says to her as he leads her back to the center of the room. Next to the table, a warm fire snaps in the fireplace.

Though her face must have said it all, Rosalina gained an embarrassed visage. Once he took his seat back at the table and with a flick of his hand, his desired page immediately sprang into sight; Rosalina couldn't help but blurt out the first thing that came to mind. Not that Rosalina had forgotten the magic she'd seen, yet there didn't seem to be a great segue back to it.

"Are you a wizard?" Jade winces at this. "Sorry, not sure how else to ask what you are."

"Bi." He jokes. "But regarding the magic, I am a Djinn. Unfortunately, entirely different magic than what cursed Phantom."

"You could have just told me, you know!" Saying this to Jade, she rubs her hand over her face, thoroughly embarrassed now.

"At least you didn't have to meet his immature stage of life," Jade says, nudging Ward jokingly.

"Oh, come on, I was like 400 hundred years old when I met you. Hardly immature. I had fun...I still have fun. If I remember correctly, I had to help you, and you needed guidance." The joking jabs continued; while they did, Rosalina counted the years back to figure out the age difference and when Ward was... born. She quickly decided she didn't want to know. However, it was not hard to guess now that the team of friends saved Jade from herself and maybe guided her to where she is now.

After all the running and the hype, a familiar hunger came to her, much like after each training session. Still, she felt the need to ask permission. Even with the sun out, she suspected the earrings would help. She tipped her head with an apologetic smile and raised a hand slightly to catch the two bantering friends' attention.

"As much help as I suspect the spell-casted items might be, I don't want to get caught feeding in broad daylight. I'm really hungry." Says almost sheepishly.

"That's..." Jade starts from one of the back rooms she has yet to see. Probably one with a computer, Rosalina realizes. "What I forgot to start with. Sorry, we might have to wait till later."

"Aren't you forgetting two things? One, I always have a supply knowing who I am friends with, and two, won't you need a stronger source to face your maker? I hope you were not thinking too far ahead and not expecting to face that truth?" Paused in thought for a second, Jade looked at Rosalina. It was evident she hadn't made that connection with Rosalina in mind.

"It's okay. I'm a new addition to your every plan. I can handle whatever you need me to. I swear." Giving that sense of peace with the plan, Rosalina asks Ward if he genuinely doesn't mind, even if they have to share. Waving her concerns off, he gets up, enters another room, and rummages around in a refrigerator in the cellar. With two medical bags of blood, one for each, she gingerly takes her own, careful not to make a mess. Her first thoughts as her teeth strain to release are of Phantom and Ward. "I wouldn't want to startle him or anything," she says, to which Ward nonchalantly closes his book for the third time that morning and calls Phantom outside, closing the door behind them.

A pained gasp releases as she lets her fangs drop. Jade gives her a soft, maybe even loving smile, probably familiar with the discomfort of holding back. Following how Jade pricks the bag, Rosalina assesses her reaction and desire for human blood instead of rushing like Jade, who draws in a large gulp, taking a third of the amount. Jade was right; she barely remembered her first time. Ultimately, it didn't surprise her that even cold and old, she could be easily more inclined to take it like this out of a natural craving.

Like a coffee drinker in the shop, Rosalina slowly savors the flavors before preparing herself for the inevitable last drops to cross her lips. Without a single spill, Jade helpfully takes their empty bags to discard them. At the same time, Rosalina went to invite Ward and Phantom back inside, only to find two large wolf dogs playing together in the snow and no ward in sight. Clearly, the two were burning off some energy, though it was preferred to be alone on a mountain; it must be confining. Since Phantom wasn't stuck in a small body, his energy was probably considerably higher.

Jade appeared beside Rosalina, out in the crisp air they mused at the playful pair. Someone would get hurt with all the tackling, open-mouthed grabs, and rolling into deep layers of snow. Soon enough, they trotted in, panting. Phantom rolled onto his back at Rosalina's feet, dusting the porch in powder while Ward turned back into himself and thumped an arm around Jade.

"Don't you wish you picked up that skill?" he asks out of breath.

"No way! That would be so cool." Rosalina's enthusiasm surprises them all. "I mean, is it like a dog or a wolf?"

"I never could learn to shape-shift, but that's because I don't have the intention behind it. What do I need to be a dog for." While she says this without a care, Rosalina lets her mouth hang open.

"Wow. I thought you, as a writer, would see all sorts of uses for that skill." Ward agrees with Rosalina.

"Maybe Sage would teach you." He offers as they head inside; only Phantom seems disinterested in returning to a lit fire and cozy indoors.

"Who is Sage? Another member of the group?"

"Yeah, she came around the same time as Jade. Lyra brought her in... that's boss lady, by the way." Rosalina was unsure when she would meet these people; she mentally repeated the names anyway to remember them all when she did. Once back inside, they sit at the table and begin building a plan. Despite never having been to Italy, the idea of going wasn't as touristy as some might think. They didn't plan on staying after, and Rosalina felt okay with that as she had to get her feet back in the doors of her job upon their return.

Less than a few weeks ago, Rosalina had been adjusting to the idea that sunlight was terrible and painful, that her life revolved around this news, yet now she felt wary of being out in the sun as if this had been years of experience, giving her these feelings. Fundamentally, this was the core way she worked: easygoing and adjusting to change quickly. Ward watched in awe as Jade pressed a calming hand over Rosalina's; Jade gently asked if everything was alright. Nodding her head, Rosalina looked back at their notes; she'd been taking them but hadn't recalled anything they said.

"Sorry, I'm listening really. I just was...I don't know what. There have been so many changes, which I'm fine with, honestly. Guess I just got a little lost in my head, paving out the info into a plan for the future. It's always been helping my family that came first, even learning more for them; if I return to work after we come back, it will be for me because helping my family only goes so far now." Knowing the hard decisions Rosalina faces, Jade caresses her fingers with her thumb.

"You'll be able to support your family in whatever ways you choose for as long as you choose to. If down the road you want to open your own café, I will help you do that. You Just got to sell books or have a big library room."

"That sounds like a wonderful idea. In the future, I need to focus on the now and helping you." In reviewing the notes, Rosalina felt more confident thanks to Jade's kind words; they had a solid plan though they knew everything could quickly go to shit as soon as they got to the country. She feels even more soothed by the peck placed upon her temple. Ward chuckled and hummed an almost approving sound as he stood up and permitted them to use a room to rest up and clean up. After all, they had run all morning and still had bits of debris they hadn't immediately shaken off.

"Oh, and Ward, we'll need to make a stop back through the city to grab Rosalina's passport...you have one, right?"

"I do, actually. I went to France for two weeks in my last year of high school. We can't go back though, can we? It's right next to where you live, and that's all gone. Isn't it dangerous?"

"Ward has a knack for getting in and out without being noticed." As the comment was said, Jade had already turned around and begun to head to the spare room, leaving Rosalina to shift, unsure for a moment before following her. Ward smiled at how she wanted to satisfy her curiosity but also wasn't going to waste the time Jade was clearly mapping out in her head. To that point, he took himself to rest while they cleaned up.

Just before eight o'clock, Ward disguised Phantom as a golden retriever; it was time to return to the city. Jade borrowed some provisions from Ward to add to what they packed. Meanwhile, Rosalina waited in anticipation to experience Ward's travel method. With a snap of his fingers, they came through a surprisingly thin grey smoke conveniently, landing in an alley that seemed to be backed up with steam from a factory. The ground hadn't even shifted beneath their feet like Rosalina had expected. Recognizing where they were, she was speechless at how ridiculously oblivious everyone was. If she had been a person looking in on the outside, she wondered if she'd have noticed.

"Huh, some things have changed," Ward says, looking at a shop that makes excellent empanadas. "Use to be an Irish place in the 80's." He seemed nostalgic as he looked at the food options on the window; he wanted to come back to eat sometime soon. Phantom shared his appetite with a bark. Jade clapped a hand on his back before saying they had to head a certain way. While Rosalina knew where they were, it was several miles from her place, and she preferred watching Jade lead the way.

Grinning at the pep in Jade's steps, knowing it was in some way a delight to be walking on the streets like a regular person. She felt it as well, but it couldn't have been the same compared to how many years Jade might have felt like a beast or something equivalent. A few blocks closer, they were just like everyone else, albeit they looked like college students taking on the nightlife. As the street to Rosalina's apartment came into sight, she stepped up to lead them the rest of the way because it would be strange if she did not let them in.

Once inside, she couldn't help but wonder about all the little things she'd brought into her home and what she would wish to bring with her forever if there was a sudden choice. It was hard to pick at a moment's glance around; without any to spare on the thought, Rosalina made for her room as she told Jade and Ward to sit if they'd like. Rummaging through a few drawers in her room before finding her passport. All except one crucial piece of pure silver she tucked in her pocket, she returned everything, including pointless papers and possessions, to the drawers; she honestly needed to prepare for a quick, lightweight departure. She internally vowed when she came back, that would be the first thing she'd do.

Exclaiming she'd found her passport, she returned to the living room. Thankfully, she had no animals to speak of and nothing keeping her here that she couldn't live without. She didn't need a longing look around before Ward did his magic, and they were gone to catch their flight.

The plane wasn't too crowded, and thanks to Ward's help, they got Phantom aboard as a service animal. While Phantom would never entirely act like an actual service dog, his guard was up as he sat in the carrier. Jade sat to Rosalina's left in the three-seat row. While Rosalina usually preferred a seat closest to the aisle, she sat between them and pressed her nervous hands down her legs.

The urge and unreasonable hunger were easiest to ignore on the streets when people were further away. It helped that, more often than not, the stench of trash or the like covered the faint aroma, but here, with the A/C circulating, she strained in her seat. Knowing how she felt walking past the flight attendant, the best choice was between two people capable of stopping her. Jade leans in and softly asks how she is feeling, to which Rosalina swallows her saliva and whispers.

"I'm fine." She didn't need to gesture around at how close everyone was. Wearing a determined expression, she removes a silver coin from her pocket, pressing it between her fingertips with a wince. Holding it with as much pained control as she had a desirous restraint to let it go. It subsides her thoughts of feeding for now, and she places it away again, after which Jade rolls a thumb over her hand.

It was this mature and robust sense of willpower that Jade admired about Rosalina. Though they hadn't discussed it, Jade suspected Rosalina's self-control was a secret power old souls had to outweigh instinct with noble intentions. Personally, Jade had always had a hard time finding control, that was until she met her family through Lyra, Sage, and Ward. Giving Rosalina a comforting peck as the flight attendants start reviewing safety instructions. Once Jade is sure Rosalina is alright, she adjusts, settles in some earbuds, and takes Rosalina free hand for part of a grueling ten-hour flight as the plane rumbles while rolling into position for takeoff.

Once the rattling of turbulence stops, Rosalina releases Jade's now relaxed hand. Ward, on his part, let them have their moment despite how delighted he was to be off the mountain and out. Unlike a hermit, his social meter wasn't capped by now; in fact, Ward seemed more than happy to be surrounded by strangers and crying children. As quietly as he could to not surprise her, he chirped up.

"So, when did the romance between you two happen? Are you why she left? How long before she left were you a thing?" It's then it clicks Ward is a curious gossip type. She gives him a slightly teasing look before offering anything, and he returns it with a pout.

"Okay, okay, actually, we only just met. Jade saved my life, but we only met once just before that. I think it was a fluke. She seemed surprised at the time and told me that she never really intended to cross paths with me. She Learned after moving to the city that I was the reason she was drawn there but didn't want to approach me."

"Really? I wonder why you; I mean not that you are not simply a dear, but that's never happened before to anyone in our group...at least I don't think it has." He puzzles for a moment, then affirms that he's pretty sure. "Not counting Dylan and Adreana, vampire and succubus. They are a dynamite pair. Mortals luring a vampire in seems a bit backward to me."

"Well, it is a little complicated, I guess. I smell like some people she knew." His eyebrows raise at this. "Wait, not like how it sounds...my great grandparents Jade saved them as well, but it went a bit different; they weren't afraid of her, gave her a home for a few years, and she felt welcomed. I reminded her of happy memories. My great grandma told me stories before she passed, but I never thought they would be true until I woke up changed."

As they spoke quietly enough not to be overheard by others, Rosalina half expected Jade to hear them and pipe in as if they were childishly gossiping away. She sat there still tuned into music that bled out of the earbuds ever so slightly. Just as Rosalina glanced at her, Jade's fingers began tapping. It was an old tune from the 80s that sounded similar to something her father used to listen to when she was growing up, though she couldn't place the name.

"How'd you take it all? You seem fine."

"I am pretty good with all of it. I never thought I'd be traveling to Italy like this, having dreams of a life I'll be living well beyond what I expected and falling for not only the most stunning woman but her friends. I've never had such close relationships that distance didn't break the foundation of a friendship. You all sound amazing to be still around for each other."

"Speaking for myself, I am pretty amazing." They laugh out, oblivious to more turbulence as they talk, until even Phantom expresses his discomfort with a whine. Reaching down, Ward pets him gently, reassuring him that he is safe. Unfortunately, what licks he receives do not change the fact that neither could let him out of his kennel. He seems to be a tidy man yet still wipes his fingers on his pants, while Rosalina knows she wouldn't mind the drool, she didn't think Ward was the type.

As soon as she thinks of how he never has even a crease out of line, she swears after a second glance that the moisture there moments ago has just disappeared. Among all his traits, he had a niche that Rosalina couldn't picture his personality without now. If

Jade didn't appear so in her head, Rosalina might have turned to her and asked if she'd noticed this about him.

Being this was how Jade looked, with her head tilted back and closed eyes, Rosalina found herself free of conversation and now silently biting her lip nervously as she looked out the window where the passing clouds seemed to allow no glimpse of what was to come. Accompanying two impressive people who didn't seem worried made her ready to go, yet as their landing drew closer, she couldn't help thinking her heart would usually be racing and her lips dry. Her skin, however, felt calm. When she licked the borders of her lips, her mind continued to reel with thoughts of the many situations they might encounter.

The plan to arrive during the daylight seemed like the safest option; old habits of overthinking set in, and Rosalina began to picture the arrival turning into a brawl as their foes wore their own sun-protective items. After all, while Rosalina trusted Jade's own experiences with her maker, it was ultimately 500 years since they interacted together. Amid watching her wring her fingers, Ward cuts through with a calm voice.

"Jade and I have faced far worse together and came out fine. This guy and his crew are nothing to worry about. We used to talk about this kind of thing all the time. He's never engaged her like he did last night, so we never handled it. I know she would express this if she were not feeling her past right now. The loss of her family has always been this hard on her."

"isn't that really just her also thinking of him and how cruel he was to her." He pauses a moment and agrees but goes on to say that Jade has more of a kind heart than a vengeful one. There was no way to fully know the thoughts and feelings that might be leading Jade, so despite not wanting to do something for all the wrong reasons, Rosalina separated her hands and accepted they were in this together not because of vengeance but to make the next 500 years safer. They didn't need a maker that tried to threaten them by looming around every corner.

"Sorry, I don't mean to seem so indecisive. I am here to help. I just don't typically find myself making a scene about anything unless it's to help others. I suppose this feels more like it is helping me, but only because I'm new to the situation."

"You might be new, but I feel you'll fit right in. I hope I'm there when Lyra meets you." He tells her that Lyra never comes to America unless they need to call her but that when she does, it ends up feeling like the whole family is together again. Knowing the threat didn't require aid from the group gathering together did make it easy to hold lighter conversations until the end of the flight. Even if she was put at ease and felt more ready to face the foreign reigning man in the shadows, Rosalina felt the looming effects on all of them the closer they got.

7

Man of the Cloth

Arriving at the airport and taking the first shuttle to the middle of the city struck the three in very different ways. Rosalina seemed to float in awe at the surreal atmosphere around her, entranced by the language and sights that danced all around. Like watching a dream play out, she marveled as if the daylight reflected off buildings and the sun sat in the sky entirely differently than back home. Ward bounced with energy that kept him hanging on every scent he crossed paths with; in a place like Italy, anything you might have had before was on a whole new level.

Jade enjoyed the pair's reactions to her homeland despite never being able to take pleasure in the same things they were now. Phantom nervously padded beside Jade as he adjusted to not being in a carrier anymore. Mentally, Jade regarded how his comfort would come in time, whereas hers, she feared, might never occur. With every alleyway or every face Jade's woeful eyes scanned, she resisted the urge to hurriedly get this whole ordeal over with.

They walked from the center of town to where the old cathedral was. Even if it had been so many years, Jade knew her clan would never have moved. She could still picture the layers of settled dust on the church pews without much effort, like it was yesterday. Getting closer, the weighted chime of the cathedral bell rang.

* * *

Jacopa could recall that night, the way Gabriel had compelled her to follow him through the city streets. Though she'd been in a daze, she still remembered the fear and sickness in her gut, knowing she had killed someone. A series of chimes signaling the early hour rang out, growing louder the closer they got. Any stray thought of Gabriel ticked at her like claws sinking deeper into her flesh and heart, dragging her back.

Though the church she'd come to with Gabriel, just minutes after draining a man of his blood, was still running, it looked as though not many people visited anymore. Treading through the center aisle by candlelight and moonlight, the wood looked worn and aged; dust was undisturbed on the pews. Slick, filth-riddled hair fell into Jacopa's face as she looked down, wishing not to be noticed by anyone. A craning man stepped past a pillar with eyes resting on Gabriel and her as they passed. His eyes were full of emeralds and sapphires, while the rest of him looked as if he could melt into the shadows. The man was dressed all in black, much like Gabriel. The man stood idle as they approached the podium and entered the open doorway beyond it.

"Who are you?" Jacopa asks after several minutes of silence, trying not to let the question shake as it comes out. He had given his name but not why they were there. As she thought on it, the only thing was to assume he had a form of persuasion over her because one minute she couldn't bear the idea of following him, and the next she was. Even before entering the main doors, there seemed to be a darkness surrounding this church that she would never have gone near willingly.

"Your maker, I already told you. I suppose it's easier to say I'm the only maker in this coven. No one here is above me." In this way, he sounded like he expected her to call him master. "It's not something to be bitter about. As I said before, you can call me Gabriel." He says coaxingly, taking her in further; they eventually enter a circular room full of lit torches. There are three paths to which she tells herself to remember the middle one as the one they use. The path heads into a large pillared room with a single throne-like chair in the far back just before a balcony staircase. Over 20 men standing and talking instantly grow silent and stare at them. Each pair of eyes had the most pure and wholesome eye colors she had ever seen. Even Gabriel has an opal look to his naturally grey irises.

It wasn't even ten minutes in, and the depth of trouble she felt being surrounded by men was enormous. Looking around, Jacopa was unsure what would happen next. Engrossed in her surroundings, Jacopa quickly loses sight of the throne. She circles on her heels to see Gabriel, leaving the room behind a door she hadn't noticed just beyond the throne against the wall under the balcony. Attempting to follow, she is ushered back by two men who stand in front of the door. Left there, it is clear Gabriel was no kind leader, yet the thought of leaving the way she came made her shake with pain. Among sneers and bitter words whispered about her being such a ragged and weak-looking girl, she took a seat on the steps, choosing not to appear daunted by the circumstance. Like schoolboys near her home, she felt it best not to engage with anyone before it was clear who, if any, were of similar character.

None of the eyes she chanced a gaze at ever looked kindly like her father's, who was all she could think of at a time like this. Those who entered the room and headed up the staircase as the hours passed hadn't bothered with showing her presence any interest. Comrades passed the time with each other, boasting on their most recent haunts or bellowing songs. Those who stood alone made her the tensest because if this coven, as Gabriel called it, did not have anyone she could bond with, she imagined she'd have a tough time proving herself.

Getting up finally, as her nerves have settled, she strides up the stairs confidently and begins to give herself the tour once at the top. Seeing sets of tables with chairs filled, she keeps walking to one of the openings closest to the staircase she'd picked. Focusing on this one rather than crossing the balcony to the other side, she slips into the torchlight hallway without anyone obviously following her. Amid the stark surroundings that lacked any sense of comfort or homeliness, Jacopa couldn't help but acknowledge the enduring nature of the stone, if only in her thoughts. It was daunting to admit this was the reality of her new life; Jacopa knew there was no going back the moment her name slipped from her lips, and now, after she'd killed the doctor's aid, it would take everything in her to learn how to never repeat such a grim act.

Some rooms sat in complete darkness, empty or with gleaming eyes watching her as she passed. In contrast, other rooms held figures in the dark with entranced women draped across the stone like a sheet as they were feeding from them, not giving Jacopa any comfort in the idea of being reformed. Forcing herself past those rooms, Jacopa quickly hid herself in the next empty room she found. Keeping to the shadows on the floor, back pressed against the stone wall of the doorway. Calming down, the pain and chills that filled her faded; however, the desire to do what she had witnessed still weighed on her.

Jacopa watched endless flickers of the torchlights before someone entered the room. A slight start came from the pale boy who looked no older than she was; she'd come to realize sleep was not drawing nearer, but it seemed this room was also taken and could not be used as her place to retreat. Getting up, Jacopa lifted her hands in surrender. Perhaps he'd be friendly.

"Sorry, I needed a spot to... it's a lot to take in." His kind expression ripped into a snarl, causing Jacopa to press her back into the wall again, slowly side-stepping toward turned into quickly exiting while trying not to listen to the furious shouts trailing from his room. Stumbling down the hall a few steps but making her way through an entrance to somewhere else, she finds the same three paths as before and takes the furthest one to find only the same in this hallway as was in the last. Halfway through the hall, she stops, her attention caught on a woman dancing with a dazed man; before she leans in, Jacopa tears her eyes away, only hearing the hums of her pleasure. The woman then whispers in his ear that he needs to return to his wife and confess his desire to her, not the church or God.

He brushes past Jacopa, too focused on exiting even as the woman gasps in delight at the sight of Jacopa. Looking at him and then the woman, she wonders if that is what all the people she'd seen were to the coven. Religious or sinners all looking for help from the church. This woman was no nun, with her pink silk and sheer fabrics barely covering her pale skin.

"Astonishing, isn't it?" The woman asks, covering herself. "Power to make them come or go as you please. I'm Enna." An Irish accent for an Irish name.

"I wouldn't say that, but I suppose it works if you find it useful." She replied, not that she planned on doing it herself, hoping Enna didn't take offense. Unfazed, Enna shrugs and ushers her to come into the room. Warily, Jacopa follows. It didn't take more than a glance to know this room was different than she'd seen where, in some, the stone looked like a coffin against the pitch-black or a slab used as a table for a feast. Enna's was a tempting bed where passion and desires were shared.

"It's a shame I can't say it works on the lot that live here. Pigs, most of them." Gesturing to rooms on either side but directing to mean the whole coven. Jacopa feels herself frown before she can cover it up and finds herself tense, waiting for another furious response to her presence. "It's alright. I thought the same thing, but Gabriel doesn't care what we do as long as we all do our dues to repay him for his gift."

To this, Enna didn't sound displeased or ungrateful; the opposite, in fact. Jacopa knew she'd need to fit in even a little if she wanted someone on her side here. Swallowing her disgust, Jacopa summons genuine thankfulness and almost a hint of joy. Introducing herself, admitting just for a second how much she appreciated being alive.

"Hi, my name is Jacopa, and It's not that I don't feel thankful to be alive. I can't imagine when someone gets used to living just by feeding and not sleeping again."

"Oh, you're one of those types. My husband was one, though he didn't last too long here." She says sweetly, not hesitating to add a bit of advice. "Listen, I'd hate to see the only other woman in the coven disappear so quickly, so I only say this to help you. Forget about feeling bad. It gets you nowhere with Gabriel, and if you don't have him, no one will hesitate to get rid of you to prove a point."

"What happened to your husband?" Jacopa asked with a gulp, unsure she needed to know the details since she could imagine. Following it with another question. "How come you're here if no one wants women around?"

"My husband was changed; he pleaded and swore he would serve Gabriel forever if he changed me too. Gabriel is the only one allowed to change people. After some time, even though I was a vampire like he asked, he still couldn't stomach what needed to be done. I urged him to respect Gabriels's gift to us since I was the one who got changed unwillingly, and even I was on board. I never could understand how he could just off himself..." She shook her head as she reflected on whatever means he'd done it and continued replacing her discontented expression with a smile. "You get what I mean, right? Like, why waste an opportunity to work alongside a powerful person and experience the thrills you never imagined before?"

"Yeah, that's a good point." Jacopa manages to say this despite her throat being dry and chilled after hearing how Enna talked about the two men, one in low regard and the other in the highest. "Still, what else is there to do without any sleep? I worked on a farm. I'd be so useful if I were busy." At this, Enna grabs up a black cloak from the flat stone bed and flutters to the hallway.

"Come, I'll show you!" draping the cloak over her shoulders, using it to hide her attire.

They walk together back to the three paths and out into the church. What sun she expected was still very low. Her body told her it was the time she usually got up to go to the well; just then, a pang of guilt sank in her gut, realizing her parents would be troubled with burdens without her. Not intending to, she'd missed everything Enna was saying.

"... it's not that we can't leave the church. It's that Gabriel has his rules. You must prove you can follow them before he lets anyone out into the city alone at night." Jacopa knew she recalled Enna saying something about how it was the guy's jobs to pass off as a bishop, but had she missed what she'd said about what the two of them would do amongst those looking for healing or guidance. Now, she spoke of rules. All of which Jacopa could do, but ultimately, the rules here would be much different than anything she ever had to follow at home.

"What kind of rules, though? Can you leave?" Jacopa asks, trying to focus on the situation at hand.

"I did once, but my husband could not control himself out there; good riddance, he died. Cowardly, I might add, facing the sun because he couldn't face the costs of being who we are now. It's because of Sebastian we were not exposed and why Gabriel has strict rules. If Gabriel had to become involved, he would have killed us both."

"Who is Sebastian?" Jacopa no longer felt the need to ask as a familiar man from earlier crossed the pews, gazing at them as if to ensure they did not cross some invisible line she suspected the rules must set. Not intending to find out if she had a warning before punishment, Jacopa felt her knees lock where she stood. His appearance hadn't changed, but now Jacopa could see him holding his hand beneath his cloak, resting on something hidden from sight. It gave the impression of a sword on his hip, which meant this man was clearly Gabriel's right-hand man and was not one to be tested.

* * *

Three long bell tolls echo above in the high vaulted ceilings, but as Jade hears a fourth, she blinks the past away; they've turned the last corner just before the cathedral, facing a blinding sun. Finally, the sight before her gives her shivers. It still stood; she knew it would, but simultaneously, she'd hoped it wasn't if only to be sure her friends wouldn't get injured. Facing them, Jade realizes they are serious in the face of the building, reminding her that they aren't just anyone. They were determined friends, and it did lighten her worries to know both were more than mere mortals.

Ward had the build of an averagely strong man, though his clean look often misled others to believe he hadn't ever needed to defend himself. Rosalina hadn't changed much in the week and a half, but her muscles were full. Her stride and shoulders were as confident as Ward's, who had done something like this more than once. The change in Rosalina since her altercation with the man in the alley was remarkable, marked by a newfound and tremendous strength coursing through her.

Jade's only concern was how much Rosalina could handle against a clan of unhesitating attackers, especially when swiftly and decisively ending them. As her maker, Jade didn't want to ask this of her, knowing someday there might be a line crossed when it might be too much too soon. Still, Rosalina deliberately confessed to her moments after landing that she and Ward had talked as if that would have surprised her with his personality. Rosalina admitted further how she thought Gabriel would be there waiting for them, a once human fear that faded by coming to her senses and trusting their plan; regardless of the outcome, she was determined that they would give Gabriel what was coming to him, what he was owed for everything.

"The sun shines into the front, so no one will be in the cathedral. His thralls go out during the day, and no one should be up up right now." Jade says while mentally collecting her senses and listing all the reasons this was supposed to work for her companions and herself.

"Well, with no sleep, someone will hear us," Rosalina says, not trying to dissuade any of them but mentioning it to encourage saying what needed saying now.

"It won't matter. Between Ward and I, we have things up our sleeve that none of them will have. With you and Phantom going together, we each will have an upper hand." Jade swept her hand over Rosalina's shoulders reassuringly, almost wishing she could see the raw instinct she knew Rosalina would use to pull through.

A soft, worn texture adorning the tall doors nearest the astragal could be seen as they silently walked up and pushed them open, easing pressure on the surrounding architecture and allowing the church to let out an exaggerated creak, stressing the buildings age. Entering directly was the only means to ensure a clear view inside, as the stained-glass windows obscured any other vantage point. The wider the doors went, the more shimmers of yellows and reds stretched along the floors to the back walls. An old man slumped on a pew, lightly snoring; he was the day priest Jade took it and was thankful the doors hadn't woken him.

Nothing, not even a hidden thrall put on guard in case of retaliations, interrupted their attempts to sneak through the door between them and the entrance to the coven. Once inside the passage, they followed each other closely until the hallway opened to the familiar room of three paths. Jade knew Gabriel was straight ahead while the other two were full of bloodthirsty, if not compelled, vampires. The most difficult would be the hand-picked three guarding Gabriel's private rooms, of which one was certain to still be Sebastian.

It wasn't out of Jade's array of expectations included in the plan that the coven would have grown over the many years. What used to be 50 to 80 men and a few women was now likely much higher. Possibly 50 for each of them. What she had forgotten over all the time away was the lack of circulation; the air was filled with a mixture of old dust, human sweat, old and new blood. The cool stone walls were the only thing to give a reprieve as if surrounding them with something to calm their nerves before unleashing a fiery display of strength and power.

"This is a terrible plan," Ward whispers as he makes a plucking motion at Phantom, slipping the disguise off the dire wolf. He shook with the transition as if letting his muscles stretch and loosen.

"Why don't you come up with a better one if you hate it so much!" she whispers back but with surprise that her friend would say something against it now of all times. Feeling Rosalina shift beside her, she could sense her intentions were still unmoved.

"Oh no, you misunderstand. I adore this plan...but that doesn't make it any less terrible," Ward says while expelling fog from his hands, ready to cause some mischief. If they thought about it, yes, it was a terrible thing to do. That truth did not stop the three of them as they stepped up to the paths they would take or keep Jade from summoning shadowy replicas of herself; nothing felt more natural and necessary. Rosalina and Phantom were in awe because they had nothing more than themselves to prepare compared to the mystics beside them.

In the Devil's Grasp

Stepping into the tunnel to the right, Rosalina and Phantom trod gently across the stone for a minute before the first rooms came into sight. Of course, Jade gave her fair warning there would be vampires that wouldn't hesitate to attack her; honestly, she didn't expect to see several heads down the torch-lit hall pop out once they had picked up the sound of either their footsteps or Phantoms breathing. He gave a deep growl at the first one to fully step out to them; instinct surged a chill over her, and then the fighting began as the bearded man lunged. Dodging to the low left of his torso, she immediately jammed her elbow into his ribs and watched him slam into the wall.

Quickly, her senses spiked as things progressed, she saw and felt everything. The way her toes pressed through her shoes into the ground, exerting as much strength to change her direction as fluidly as possible. Dodging a few of her attackers only to tap off the walls and hit a clean shot. Tearing one after the other open, not stopping to see if they stayed down. Jade's shadow replica clotheslined, tripped, or smothered a few men, making it easier to take them down before passing through the stone wall and reappearing deeper into the mass of enemies; even more so, Phantom seemed to be handling the ones that stood back up with the pure force of his claws or jaw.

Covered in rubble and blood, Rosalina faced the last five, who had been smart enough to wait back but not wise enough to make a plan of attack. Taking a moment to see that Phantom was still close, she could see the ferocity they had paved so far. There must have been twenty men taken down, if not more, and four more men and a woman were in front of her. All five came at Rosalina; in a blur, she'd broken one's leg and another's arms, cracked a jaw, ripped open the stomach of one, and grabbed the woman by her head.

A hiss followed by a clawing at her hand made her lift her arm and smack the woman's skull down as hard as possible. They were all in unison, getting up and coming repeatedly; even with Phantom's help, there wasn't enough time to hit any of them with lethal blows. Just as Rosalina was sure she'd fail to clear the tunnel, the smokey figure in Jade's likeness slipped out from around the five like it had formed a plan to come up from behind them. Soundlessly, it came floating downward and quickly snapped the neck of the first man in its way. He'd been the most difficult snapping his arms back to normal when Rosalina thought she had twisted them enough to break them.

While distracted by the sudden attack, Rosalina didn't hesitate to pick up the one dangling his broken leg up slightly. She saw the others fighting off the shadow and Phantom but focused on the flailing struggle before her. She settled it by slamming her fist into him so hard she felt it collide with the wall. Her hand sank into the chest cavity.

Two more bodies fell behind her, making the woman clamor at her to have sense, to leave before this all got worse by attacking her master. After a hard yank, Rosalina freed her hand, knowing if she let this one flee or intervene in Jade's fight, she could be to blame if the whole plan failed. When she turned to face the woman and saw her already pinned by the shadow feet lifted off the floor, Rosalina added her own grip on her throat. The shadow fell like fog and then turned away, making its way up the hall and fading through the wall, evidently having somewhere else it needed to be.

"It's long overdue for your maker to meet his end," Rosalina said. With a crushing grip on the woman's neck, Rosalina could feel the desperate struggle of nails digging into her wrist as she fought to free herself and protect the man they had come to kill. At the audible snap, Rosalina's adrenaline-like haze staggered to halt as the woman in sheer clothes hovered just above the floor until Rosalina let her go and drew her shaking hand closer to her chest. Rosalina wasn't blinded with rage, but her actions were all in a quick response to any attempt to hurt, catch, or escape her. Immense feelings of growing power and lack of control began to battle within, but what really called out in her was what told her to keep moving, so she followed the slight incline of the hallway until it opened into a space with stone tables and benches.

Ward waited for the fog he'd fed into the tunnel to reach far enough ahead before transforming into a vaporous form without someone guessing where he might solidify next to strike. Next to Jade's shadow, it was not likely that anyone could find him in the gaseous form in time to land a blow. Being like this and able to openly use magic, he felt free, almost youthful, but it didn't distract him from what he knew needed to be done. A few whispers stirred, mentioning a commotion in the other tunnels while some waved at the fog, expecting that to help clear it, it only grew thicker.

Jade's shadow and Ward only attacked when no visibility was left; suddenly, screams filled the hall. Despite being almost too easy this way, Ward stayed as he was. Ward could swing his arm through three people one moment, and his blow would collide with someone the next. In this case, everything he had on his person could melt and solidify as needed, not just himself.

Ward didn't have the strength to kill bare-handed, but he did have silver scimitars that he could manipulate in the fog along with himself. Unable to decipher when or where the blades would appear, each vampire fell with their limbs severed. There were no indecisive vampires here; none not full of rage and seeking to kill the attacker, so none would survive. Jade knew Ward well enough he wouldn't be forced to kill if he decided he would not kill an unprovoking being.

Disappointedly, he struck down the last manic vampire as he swung blows into the fog wildly. With the last man down, he stepped solidly on the ground again, striding up and out just in time to see Rosalina emerge from where her path had led her. It wasn't a surprise but a relief to see her and Phantom making it safely to where Jade had said they would end up.

Jade was sure as soon as the others made their moves, she'd need to be already or nearly done with whoever occupied the main room. She hurried down the longer-than-she-remembered middle path, finding it had more than three guards. Before anyone who did see her could move, Jade made quick work of at least two vampires. A wave of desire to surrender tried to fill her, but she shook it off just in time to move, so an incoming fist collided with a pillar behind her.

Gabriel would never compel her again; of that, she was sure. Her determination was unwavering. The man she had dodged and many, if not all of the men here, were stirred to fight her or compelled more likely. Instead of turning to face a vampire coming up from behind her, she runs forward, drawing whoever it was closer toward another vampire.

Dropping low, Jade swept her foot full circle; as expected, they avoided it easily but missed her rising up to grab their collars and yank them into each other. They are not even close to getting up when she finishes them. After them, it was a full-on fight; every man from the top balcony climbed down to have a hand in taking her down. Allowing a numbing sensation to fill her as her instincts told her she couldn't hold back as her brethren were fighting in the name of Gabriel.

Recognizing most of the faces made it easier to be cold; the ones she didn't know would bother her the most later. With an overwhelming difference in skill, even without the aid of her shadows that she'd split up to help the others, she had cleared the way to her true goal. The three she expected to be guarding the door were down to one. Sebastian glared at her in hatred, and a snarl crossed his face.

"The prodigal child returns." He all but hisses, unsheathing his sword. It shined with a silver she had often seen cut down any vampire that Gabriel had become fed up with. Without a weapon of her own, Jade closed the space to give him less swinging power. He spun on his heel in a flash, gliding the sword upward and causing her to change to dodging. "You can't beat me, child. You should never have been a choice to Gabriel."

"Does it bother you that he wanted me to be his right hand instead of you?" Jade said mockingly, knowing that that position had never mattered to her, but that Sebastian would get agitated. His grip tightened on the hilt, and he lunged.

"Like he would really have ever made you his second. His bitch maybe, even if he always had a more than unnatural obsession with you." He'd forced her back down the steps to the throne and further away from the door. "Look at you, still the same filth that came in that night. He should have killed you with your parents when he had the chance. Once a trai-aackkk. "His words fell short as a black shadow forced itself into his mouth, nose, and ears. Sebastian choked; as his sword slipped from his grip, Jade swiftly grabbed it and swung hard enough to sever his head from the rest of him.

Sensing not only her fight but the other's fighting had also subsided, allowing her to call her other shadows back.

"You're wrong," Jade says, looking down at the blade reflecting the scene. With creaking from the only door in the room, Jade's head springs up.

"Yes, in many ways he was. You have always been the better choice for one." Jade raised the sword as her shadows came to her side. Gabriel swished away his cloak so matter of factly it barely seemed like he was nervous at all. It was strange to see the same man who once never changed, having cut his hair to a more modern style, short all but a few inches on top and combed in a way that kept with his priest façade. "Only you would find a way to show up here in the daylight. There are not many sources for those types of items. It's a shame how little it took for my men to go down, but we both know I'm the only master in this coven."

"Not anymore. Why can't you just accept I don't want any of this!? What am I to you?" she'd had enough of this back and forth with Gabriel; however, she didn't want him to take the shadows for anything less than what they were a diversion to keep Ward and Rosalina's presence hidden for now. Gabriel grayed a little at the question.

"Not what but who...you were someone to me." He faced her unguarded as his thoughts determined what he would say next. "You recall what I shared with you about my sister?"

"You said she died because of your secret." Shocked that he might be giving her more than he'd ever given her.

"A half-truth, really. I was changed and couldn't imagine living on without my dear Édith. I wanted her to join me in this curse. Ultimately, I had to kill her because she didn't understand the potential behind the change. I should have given her more time to adjust, but I worried about the secret getting out. When I saw you, I thought it was a second chance, and then you had to go and defile it with your sinful advances on your disciple. She'd have run away by now. Nonetheless, now I know you are no Edith. My dearest sister would have never abandoned me like you did. I offered you everything over and over. When I killed your parents, I hoped you might have realized what I was trying to give you."

"Why on earth would I be your sister? You mean Like reincarnated?" Jade was sure she had never thought of this scenario when imagining facing Gabriel once and for all. Her guard was lowered as she heard his explanation, but she brought the tip of the sword back up as the truth sank in, glaring at him the more she felt the true meaning of her existence lift the weight she'd carried all this time. While she was at fault for her own decisions and the lives she'd taken, it was not solely her fault. "You did all this to me to pretend I was your sister!"

"It's irrelevant now. Once, you looked like Edith in my eyes, but now I'm done with you." He snarled, thrashing out his teeth as he leaped at her, deflecting the sword without much effort. Jade hadn't used a sword in such a long time; shaking off the rusty feeling, she pulled the hilt back, smacking Gabriel in the jaw bluntly. Not struck hard enough that he lost balance, but his teeth didn't land where their strike intended.

Jade felt her neck tighten, nearly expecting her throat to be torn out. The sword would have to be an advantage, but being as close as they were now wasn't helping. Jade and Gabriel went head-to-head, blow after blow, until there was an opening. They parred for minutes until Jade could find a gap in Gabriel's defense and struck so hard at his knee that it broke, and he dropped. As satisfying as watching him struggle to keep his leg from giving out and not look weakened was, she knew he couldn't be stopped with just this.

"Why do you resist me?" he asked, his voice filled with pain. "I've shown you your mortal parents weren't to live forever like us, your disciple was too weak and easy to frighten away, and I've told you I would have given you everything if you had just let us be family. Why do you refuse me when you are so alone?" Gabriel's eyes widened at her when he heard what Jade saw. A primal growl escaped a snarling Rosalina approaching from behind him. Rosalina had leaped off the balcony to land behind Gabriel, yanking his head back and locking it in her arms. Ward was coming, but his magic was already at work with fog-like shackles holding his arms wide-open and pulled back.

"She is not alone." Rosalina seethed lowly, rage simmering in her eyes. Having heard everything he'd said and with her reaction, Jade was surprised Rosalina had enough control to hold back her rage and leave her the opportunity to finish him off herself. For all of his distance before, Phantom made his presence just behind her known with a howl in agreement. "I should just kill you, but it's not my right. Jade deserves this moment."

Jade didn't need to think about it to know she was ready to kill her maker. Ready to rid Italy of the worst kind of monster in the shadows. Gabriel pulled franticly to free his constraints until Jade swung the sword, careful not to stand too close and wound Rosalina. His head rested separated in Rosalina's arms as his body stopped struggling; the magic that held him in place disappeared, letting the headless body fall forward.

"Thank you, guys. I could have been fighting him for a while. He was only moments away from popping his knee back and over-powering me. I'm glad I wasn't alone, I mean." Jade says to them. Rosalina did her best to look at her rather than feel disgusted at the head she was awkwardly holding. Nodding her head, Jade encourages her to just drop it. Both of them regarded Ward, who was up to something, as fog filled the room from the balcony and tumbled down the steps toward them.

"We are gonna want to clear the tunnels." Realizing his intentions, Jade ushered Rosalina and Phantom out. He had a valid point; there was no time to waste. A fire ignited brightly in the once torch-lit tunnels as they approached the main exit just past the three paths. While they waited, they covered their noses with their shirts to lessen the smell of bodies burning. Phantom whined and laid down to cover his nose with his paws. After the fires stopped, Jade requested that they give her a minute, and she'd be back.

"His private quarters were just below the balcony; he might have kept some interesting or useful things. I know it's silly, but I guess once a pirate, always a pirate." Looking shocked and slightly amused at this piece of information about Jade's history, Rosalina says she doesn't mind. Ward shrugged and said he hoped it didn't get burned up. Jade stopped at the door that had become blackened by the fire, yet she found everything untouched upon opening it.

The few valuable possessions that he had were weapons that they wouldn't be able to travel with. If he had started with anything like them, maybe they would be in a different situation right now. Jade guessed he didn't know how to wield them, just liked to keep them, seeing how it's impossible to train if no one else can get stronger with you. On his desk were maps and papers of old riddles like he liked finding lost items or maybe he was searching.

Either way, none of the papers or maps were something she'd keep. Making her way back, feeling she'd wasted time looking for no reason, she stopped. A scene became painted in her mind as she looked at a stone slab with names carved into it. At the top was her born given name with a line drawn through, probably given after her first disgrace of running away.

The second name on the list was similarly drawn through, but hers wears a newer mark of Gabriel's claws. She imagined he had come back from destroying her house when he did this. Beneath the unfamiliar name, Simone was Sebastian's, not new but made many years after Jade's name had started the list. Sebastian was a devoted man who was never a choice until Gabriel was let down too many times, even once by someone named Simone, whom Jade felt it was odd to never have met before with how close in age the top two names were made.

Beneath the board of trusted vampires sat a picture of a woman who did look a lot like Jade, except Jade had a very Italian jawline. In contrast, this woman was more Romanian in Gabriel's likeness. His alter space for her was covered in debris, candles, and more parchment with scribbled names on pages with details beside the names. Who was he looking for, not her? She'd never heard of these names.

Scanning everything on the self, she found a scroll with a letter that expressed a great desire to offer information if it would save them. It detailed their own experience and how the one who made them also left whoever they were to fend for themselves in a complicated situation. Unsure of what to make of it, Jade puts the scroll back and ponders over it as she leaves. Seemed like he was searching for his maker after all this time

"Find anything?" Ward chirps as she returns to them. Jade shrugs but replies.

"Nothing of importance to us." Kneeling to Phantom, she pets him before telling him and Ward they would need to disguise him again. The elderly priest was awake and adjusting the books in the pews when leaving the back room, giving Jade an idea to which she immediately walked over to the old priest. She didn't think her plan would fail, even with a dog present.

"Sir," she spoke up, inviting the man to look her in the eyes. "I've just run a thorough inspection." She had not, but he nodded his head and waited for her to give her report. Hating telling such a lie to an elder of the church, Jade pauses but ultimately continues, knowing it's for the best. "This place is to be closed for good. My crew and I are boarding it up this morning, and no one shall be allowed to trespass. A notice will be sent in the mail, but please report the loss of the church to your people and convince them you can serve elsewhere from now on."

Faint tears swelled in his eyes as he looked around. It had been a long time coming from the acceptance Jade saw. It was plain to see how old and rundown the church had become; she suspected her maker's compulsion on the priest had been lifted, or the man had been holding on to old memories for so long that as he faced her, he sniffed lightly before bowing his head and bidding his farewell. Rosalina stepped closer, her mouth gaping.

"Well, I suppose we have some work to do then?" Ward says, ushering out what little people were still inside as politely as possible, leaving the two of them to speak freely.

"Did you hypnotize him?" Rosalina asks, unafraid of being overheard seeing Ward exit the building and close the doors behind himself and the last person leaving. Perhaps to ensure they all left and closed the gates that sat open when they arrived as they did whatever work they could to close the church down for good.

"No, but Gabriel could have. I simply encouraged him to look at me as I spoke and listen. He has probably worked long enough to take me at my word." Jade smiles lightly, taking Rosalina's hand, showing how not offended she was by the suggestion of using the power of persuasion.

"So, you were a pirate?" Rosalina asks, changing the topic away from Gabriel. They walked to a closet together so Jade could pull out equipment like hammers and nails.

"You did such a great thing for me, and I'm so thankful. I haven't explained much about myself and the long history I have. Gabriel isn't even the worst, to be honest." After several moments of handing each item to her and taking a few things herself, Jade says, "But yes, I left piracy abruptly right before I met Ward and the gang. It was not all that it was cracked up to be."

"You had adventures?" Rosalina asks, wondering if at least she saw the world.

"None so grand as I had when traveling on land helping people with the group and certainly nothing like we have had today." After returning to the front doors again, Jade asked Rosalina something in return. "How do you feel? I mean, with what you had to do and who you had to hurt."

Rosalina set the tools on a bench lining the windows near the door. They had no wood yet to do as Jade said they would after all and faced Jade feeling just a little weighted by her question. She had tried to push past it or force it to become like a hazy memory that would pass in time, but as she thought about it, she felt sad not to know who each person was and if they truly deserved it.

"At first, it seemed like they were just protecting their space, and then they were manic. I was doing whatever my body needed to make it through. The last one, she was devoted, really the only one that spoke up, but I could tell she was driven to fight me."

"She? Hmm. I wouldn't beat yourself up over her. The only other woman in the coven was definitely devoted to Gabriel. I think she would have cut off her own head for him." Jade says although she wished she'd have seen Enna for herself. "I'm sorry you had to do all that; as much of it was for me, I am glad you will not have to worry about Gabriel as I have."

"It was such a haze like all adrenaline... to be honest, I'm surprised I could even control myself."

"But you did," Jade says proudly, showing Rosalina she was just as happy she'd managed to. "You have a kind nature to you. That is not often the type of people that become supernatural. Perhaps that is what separates you from the rest."

Jade feels a rush of emotion seep through their connection as Rosalina embraces her. Jade melts into the touch and wraps her arms around her, realizing how relieved she feels. Forgetting as they held their embrace about the old sentiments for the place they were in and the task at hand for just a moment to bask in something so peaceful. It couldn't last forever, as the church groans once Ward re-enters. Its pause and finish echoes, giving his apparent desire to not interrupt them no such luck, making them chuckle as they separated.

"I uh managed to get us some wood." He says, pointing outside. "They had some logs around the side, but I had to make it more for our use."

Once outside, Rosalina could see what he meant. They needed planks, and the wood piles were too neatly trimmed to have been made that way by hand; he clearly used his powers. Jade found a window cleaning ladder they would need. Setting the tools and nails down, they start covering windows and driving the nails into the structure. In the meantime, a disguised Phantom lay in the sun or ran around, only coming to pant for water when he needed it.

Three or four boards in total crossed each window. The supply didn't dwindle as they worked; after reaching the sides, especially with how tall the front windows were, Rosalina suspected Ward was helping multiply the resource as they went along. The last thing they covered was the door to the coven on the inside and the main entrance of the cathedral. To which Jade looked saddened; in all fairness, everything she'd ever known had been changed in just half a day.

If Rosalina didn't know better, she might have guessed it was about good and fond memories; however, she took her expression as one that contemplated religious or historical benefits to the church staying open. This was not the last Jade would hear of the church, as Jade needed to reach out to one or two contacts who could manage the shutdown from behind the scenes; either way, Rosalina was confident that Jade knew all that needed following up. Rosalina wondered what people would miss most: prayer or how it stood after all this time as she looked over their finished work. Rosalina tried to ease her mind by nudging Jade when they were all done and placing the extra tools on the wood pile.

"People will be curious, and tales always outlast a place. Someone will see its beauty and take pictures, I'm sure." Rosalina said, omitting how she'd known people to break into places to get the pictures they wanted. Jade grinned at the thought. With everything put out of sight, some thanks to Ward, they began leaving. Only then did they hear the jangle of a chain, making Jade spin in surprise.

"Here, let me." Jade threw out her hands hurriedly, taking Rosalina aback. Ward gave her a half smile and spoke to Rosalina as if he knew the speed and concern Jade showed needed explanation.

"Thanks. Jade knows I dislike looking at these, let alone holding one." He let it slip from his fingers into her hands. She then wrapped the gate bars and brought the end with the open lock to join with the rest. Looking up at the cathedral one last time, the sun behind a tower, the boards across the windows and doors, and the closed gate, it looked like it was meant to be abandoned.

"Makes sense being who you are. Are there any Djinn ever free from the start?" Rosalina asks.

"I was actually. I was born of two Djinn. They did their best to keep me free, but I was trapped one day, and it took just under a century to get free again, thanks to my brother." How he said this shook her, unable to imagine the fear he had endured, but she admired that he could be open about it. Was being someone important to Jade really enough for him? They hadn't even gotten to figure out what they were yet. It was a shame that they were in a place known for big romantic gestures and would be leaving to return home soon.

"How old were you? You've been trapped and freed, yet you have never come here?" Rosalina asked as they walked the way they came through the city.

"Young, but no, with all my masters and any trips I've made to see more of the world, I've never been exactly here. It's a shame because the delicious-smelling food here is amazing!" Ward was leaning into the fragrances. Looking at Jade, Rosalina raised a questioning eyebrow.

"I mean, it's not like he doesn't get hungry, and we did just do all that?" she says pleadingly on his behalf.

"We only have a few hours before our flight home leaves...fine, I suppose. Where should we go first, then?" Ward beamed and sprang off to find out what in all the food around he wanted to try. Rosalina happily swept up one of Jade's arms and leaned in, resting her head on her shoulder as they walked. That was all she needed, and Rosalina knew Jade felt the same when a soft hand rested on hers in return. They couldn't stay long; returning home meant returning to work soon, and neither of them was sure that nothing would happen once life went on.

What unsettling feelings in Jade were pushed aside and replaced by sad visions of the past? Each building along the way was a place in her village she used to visit, and some looked nearly the same in shape or size while others had either doubled or been made taller over the years. By following Ward, eventually a just as excited Rosalina, she'd been led in the same direction as her past originated. While she didn't want to feel saddened, she knew they were near somewhere she hadn't ever had the heart to see again. Ward and Rosalina appeared, food in hand, breaming with flavorful pleasures, but they paused at the gloom setting on her face.

"Jade, what's wrong?" Rosalina asked shakily. Even Phantom whined, worried for her.

"Would you guys mind if we went somewhere before we leave? I could go alone if-"

"Of course, lead the way." Ward's response was immediate and resolute, cutting her off before she undoubtedly thought other- wise. Vulnerability crested Jade's facial features like a wave washing over the surface of her emotions, which neither Rosalina nor Ward intended to turn away from Jade now. Ward motioned that they would follow, then looked to Rosalina, wondering if she had any clues about where they were going.

Any sternness, comfort, and passion they were used to slipped away as they followed Jade through the quiet streets. Rosalina re- flected on the layers of Jade's character, including the time she met Jade in the diner; Rosalina never witnessed this facet of Jade's personality.

The vulnerability that now creased Jade's eyes into a woeful ex- pression was a revelation, stirring the deep affection and admiration Rosalina already felt for her. From their first meeting, she had been struck by Jade's powerful presence. Her authoritative voice and unwavering resolve had initially painted a picture of a strong and in- dependent woman. It was a side of Jade that had earned Rosalina's respect.

In the days following her change, Rosalina had come to appreciate Jade's comfort and honesty when she'd learned something new about being a vampire. In moments of doubt or uncertainty, Jade's calming presence had consistently been a balm for Rosalina's anxieties about returning to the bustling city. Her gentle words and listening ear had created a safe space for sharing thoughts and feelings. And then there were those times when Jade's passion shone brightly.

Rosalina had seen Jade throw herself into writing projects, rising up to fight her maker for all the right causes, and stand firm in what she believed, but never force the choice on Rosalina if she wasn't ready. It was inspiring to witness Jade's unwavering dedication and the fiery determination that fueled their victory. Yet the side that Jade revealed now touched Rosalina's heart. The tears that brimmed Jade's eyes now were a stark reminder that behind the strong, calm, and passionate exterior was a person with her own fears and insecurities. It gave Rosalina hope in her own future that after 600 years of one hardship after another, Jade still had her humanity.

Whatever lay ahead, she admired Jade's courage for holding onto it alone for so long and was grateful for Jade's trust in them. If Ward had known what Jade endured here, maybe he had never pictured her nostalgia or known the distance she'd kept from the life she lost. Rosalina did imagine that Jade had been swept far away until she'd lost her family. If the same city they came to fight Gabriel was the same that was once her village, Rosalina couldn't imagine the internal struggle it must have been for Jade.

Looking out from the top of a small hill, the road took a bend beyond which Rosalina felt in her gut that was their destination. Jade's family home or something just as sentimental. Not knowing what to expect, Rosalina felt her hands shake anxiously in anticipation.

Rosalina tucked them inside her pockets and took in the view from atop the hill for a moment.

Save for the sight of one delicate food Rosalina instantly knew would appeal to Jade due to its rawness, all of Rosalina's attention had been on Jade. Good and bad outcomes of offering it to Jade stirred though. Rosalina hoped for a smile as a reward for giving her some of home. Still, she knew nothing about the food and if whatever the dish was would feel like home or just another reminder that raw was their only craving anymore.

Ward spotted her interest as they began passing the vendor's shop. Falling back momentarily, he picked up a few for her and paid the man quickly so they both didn't have to leave Jade's side. They needn't worry, as Jade seemed momentarily frozen by the view until Ward handed Rosalina the plate with a knowing smile. Feeling slightly encouraged, Rosalina waited for an opportunity to present itself as they began their descent.

9 |

Heading Home

In the city, they mainly enjoyed food and wine, all to Ward's liking. From Parmigiana Di Melanzane to German imported Riesling. Jade did like the Riesling even if she had some history with Germany. While Jade's surface thoughts were trying to focus on these little things, she knew the feeling in her stomach was the sign of thoughts churning much deeper. Leading the way down a road that she once ran through long ago, the others followed beside her, surprisingly without hesitation.

The trek was over in no time; they'd reached the top of a small hill. Though the other two looked at the same bend in the road, they didn't know what lay just beyond. Of all the rivers Jade had visited and listened to, the one just ahead sounded the most like returning home. Still standing, now finished, a near reflection of the image in her mind, the Ponte alle Grazie bridge seemingly awaiting her return.

Stepping onto the bridge gave Jade a feeling of proud completion, proof her father had been there and lived on until his mortal life was over. Pausing midway across, Jade rested her arms on the railing and looked it over, wondering which pieces, if any, she could tell were worked on by her father before setting her interest on the waters flowing under it. Rosalina and Ward joined her in tandem, though Ward faced away from the water as he indulged his appetite, sometimes giving Phantom pieces to eat. At the same time, Rosalina gently nudged Jade, offering her a piece of beef carpaccio.

"Thank you." She said gingerly, picking up the raw meat, half expecting it to drip from her fingers; it held intact until it was in her mouth. Only then did it become so delicate it melted at the temperature change. Giving an impressed mewl at Rosalina's excellent choice given their particular preferences. Cleaning her fingertips, she expresses herself, knowing they were curious but polite enough to let her come to them. "It's beautiful. I never got to see it finished...or I should say I was afraid to come back here and be seen."

"I understand. What it feels like to leave a family you wish you didn't have to." Rosalina hadn't meant to say it out loud, but she did feel like she knew what Jade must have gone through. "It's different, I know, but I once worried about running into people I couldn't convince I was doing the right thing. I wasn't sure I was far enough away from my family that they couldn't force me to return to working for the family business and eventually marry a man. Despite how sure I was, they disliked my life choices. I had no doubt they wanted me to be a low-cost worker or push their ideals on me until I changed my mind."

"Really, your own family?!" Ward asked, unaware of the prejudice and unwavering opinionated family history Rosalina told Jade about. Wiping his face clean, he turned to look out across the water, seemed to marvel at its beauty, and then looked at them with a curious interest. Rosalina explained her family affairs, sharing that she understood the struggle to put significant distance between those who hurt her and the life she wanted. Jade had not only run away eventually from a coven but, since being changed, constantly felt like she couldn't be seen by the people of her village who believed she'd died. Jade chose to distance herself from a life familiar to her because they wouldn't be able to accept her, which is why Rosalina explained that, oddly, it was similar.

"A few cities from home is not as great a distance as going across the seas. I never traveled to other states, so New York always felt smaller than I imagined." Rosalina added after the brief story.

"And now?" Jade asks with a glint in her eyes, which might have been a half-knowing question.

"Aside from the distances we have gone since knowing you, I came to a moment of realization back when I was moving into the place I'm at now. I was nearly invisible in a sea of people, and my life was speeding by. I needed to focus on the people and places I was in and stop freezing my life to worry. I'm sure someone will be looking for me someday, but I can only hope that it's one of the better of the bunch."

"That's a wise way to look at it, but are they a danger to you?" Ward gasped as he seemed to picture thugs. Both women chuckled, but Rosalina shook her head.

"Nothing like that. After my father passed, my mother turned bitter. She and others had spiteful words to say when I came out. It took stepping away for me to realize how much they misuse or take for granted everything in this world. I don't know where it started, honestly. My grandmother and those before her were sweet, always open-minded." She shrugged and looked at Jade, bringing it back to her. Rosalina knew it was Jade's parents and neighbors that she avoided during her time here. No one could recognize her now; she wanted Jade to see that. Having an idea, Rosalina pressed her lips together, wondering where they could find something so freeing to do, even just for a minute. This spot had a few kids kicking a ball around, but further down, she spotted something and told them to wait where they were.

"Here, pick one." She says as she returns from behind them. In her hands sit three different colored kites. Both looked surprised, but with a brimming smile, Jade reached out for a green kite. Ward looked between the remaining colors and plucked a yellow one from the options. An orange-red one remained for Rosalina, and she immediately unfurled it, ensuring the string wasn't tangled.

Following her lead, she could tell they hadn't done anything so ridiculously pointless and human in such a long time. Indeed, if it had not been for a good windy day and the pieces of jewelry to protect them from the sun, they would not have the fortune of this moment. With this in mind, Rosalina cast the kite into the air and watched in awe as it kicked high into the air instantly. The string slid through her fingertips and grew taut whenever she willed it, depending on the strength of the wind or where she was.

On or off the bridge, they all managed to keep the kites in the air. Reflecting in the river as they stared high were the three colors. Where some kids chased the kite's reflections, others ran in circles, giggling around reaching upward; only one or two kids occasionally sought to play with Phantom, who leaped and bounced through the water, not avoiding them but not playing as rough as he had with Ward back at his home. Jade froze when she noticed one girl standing on the side facing the sky, lips wobbling and hands pulled close to her chest. Her tiny eyes were brimming with tears, though nothing seemed to have caused them.

"Why don't you give it a try?" Jade offered, and when the little hands hadn't moved, she knelt to put the string even closer in reach and offered again. She took it nervously but instantly filled with the same thrill as everyone else. Rosalina and Ward offered the same to other kids and stepped aside to watch from beside an old, sturdy tree. Jade pressed a hand gently on the trunk, wearing a smile bigger than Rosalina had yet to see before.

Rosalina explained she had received them from a cart; no payment was needed as they often were used and given back. She didn't know much of the language but managed, and it helped that the person could tell she wasn't from there and persistently gave her the three she had and waved off her money. Jade went to the stand, deposited a large tip in the jar on the cart, and spoke to the attendant. After a few gestures towards the children at play, she returned and said they could leave, knowing the kites would eventually be fetched.

Making it back to the airport with plenty of time to spare, they spoke aimlessly, occasionally bringing up the day's events when no one was nearby, sometimes anything that came to mind either to Rosalina or Ward. They didn't know each other all that well, but both could agree that they should after such a big trip and fight. Rosalina told him mostly anything he asked about where she grew up, what her family did to make her leave, and even why she wasn't mad at Jade for changing her life so much.

While they waited in a quiet corner for the plane to arrive, Rosalina wondered why Ward insisted on returning by plane, knowing that his only limitation was to familiarize himself with their destination. Jade had been happily observing as Rosalina and Ward got to know each other until this topic arose. Rosalina couldn't help but notice the shift in Jade's demeanor and began to worry that she might have touched on something sensitive. Phantom, sensing the unease, lifted his head within the open-doored carrier.

"I began this practice after gaining my freedom. My youthful naivety as a Djinn led me to believe I had all the time and power in the world. I didn't realize the need to protect myself from those who might exploit my magic. A greedy man eventually found me and, with powers I had never expected, ensnared me with cuffs, binding me to a bottle. Realizing how many signs I had left of my magic and abilities haunted me. I vowed to leave no such traces again." Ward explained. He might have been disappointed looking back as he said this, but Rosalina felt a wave of anger in herself at his capture. Having an empty vessel meant someone had been set free, only for the remains to become Ward's jail. "If we left to come here in my home or yours, then we could return just the same, but because we flew, we must return the same."

"I understand your caution, but won't it trouble you that we'll return directly to your place from the airport? We entered my home but never exited." Rosalina asked, finally understanding the mutual protectiveness Jade and Ward shared.

"It's a situation easily explained to any interested observers. They simply missed you. If I hadn't ensured the curtains were drawn, and someone had spotted the magic, we would be in far greater danger. Similarly, if someone claimed to have seen me at home in the morning but not later, I'd say they must have missed me, even if by mere minutes. Not everything I do has to be perfectly normal; the key is to avoid getting caught again." He concluded with a reassuring grin, signaling to Jade that the question was not as unwelcome as she thought.

Rosalina nodded, finding this explanation reasonable; their flight was a paper trail scenario, after all. She didn't need heightened senses to tell Phantom had a greater need to make it home again before she did, to replenish his energy with food he had hunted or that Ward provided. Although Phantom didn't appear excessively worn out, he was notably less bothered by the carrier this time, likely due to some fatigue. She suspected that she and Jade would rest upon their return and consider traveling at night to her home.

Rosalina figured this would be the plan because the right thing to do was to give the jewelry Ward had lent them back, ensuring they were available for someone else in need. It didn't escape her that working at the diner would be feasible during the day if she kept the earrings. A tinge of sadness came with the realization that she had let herself forget the limitations so easily with the jewelry protecting her. Working the night shift as she always had echoed and aligned with what Ward had said, Rosalina knew she must endure to keep her life as normal as possible.

Picking up the same routine was the safest choice. Of course, it would cut into nights with Jade, but it would also be the most plausible because, as Ward said, she must do what is the easiest to explain away. Working all day yet going out and coming back throughout the night, someone would wonder when she slept and begin to ask too many questions. Then, as if reading her mind rather than sensing the emotions, Jade's soft gaze held Rosalina's; amber eyes melted the worries, reminding her of the comfort and support that Jade offered at their campsite.

Ward slipped away after an intercom reported that their flight was delayed to speak to someone and returned with first-class tickets. He laughed off Jade's attempt to reimburse him, saying that they would likely need privacy after how much energy was spent at the cathedral. Rosalina knew the extra space would feel better in the long run, but thanks to Jade's shadow and Phantom's aid, she didn't even feel like she'd reached her limit yet. Recalling how the long hours in the woods took much more out of her.

Returning to the States the next afternoon, they dipped into a nearby alley and disappeared to Ward's home. Despite the warming AC, the windows were covered in snow; there seemed to be no chance that opening the door, they wouldn't find a pile at least halfway high pressed against the door as well. Flicking on a light and letting Phantom free and in his own form again, it all seemed as it was before they left.

Ward magically lit the fire from a slow spark to a quick blaze as if not to surprise Phantom or cause damage to the home from the drastic change in oxygen or heat. Having not closed his eyes once on the ten-hour flight and looking worn, Rosalina assumed he lit it this way to save time for the comfort of his bed. He eyed his room, then the pair of them, until a yawn escaped. Jade ushers him to go and get some rest as light laughter rumbles between them until Jade rests a hand on Ward's shoulder.

"I know we've been through enough that I can always count on you, but I really need to thank you for what you've done for me. Rosalina and I would have gotten lucky to do what we all did without trouble." Though he shrugs it off, they share a meaningful hug. Pulling back, Jade continues. "We're gonna borrow these for a little bit longer if that's alight."

Jade plays with the jewelry in her ear, but it looks more like a silent conversation between them to Rosalina. He chuckles and says to take as long as they need in a way that sounds to have multiple meanings. Curious about what it all means, she excitedly asks when the door Ward slips through closes. Softly caressing her cheeks, Jade says nothing despite Rosalina giving her even more pleading in her eyes and a pouting lip.

"you've certainly become even more adorable, but you'll have to come with me if you really want to know." In that, Jade could have meant Rosalina had warmed up to her, which she had, although it surprised her if she thought about how hard that usually was for her. After moving to Hell's Kitchen two years ago, she'd barely made any acquaintances, let alone any friends. As if to confirm this, she realizes that Christmas was in a few days, and she had not a single plan with anyone. Around Jade and Ward, though, maybe it would feel something like the holiday was supposed to.

"If I join you, will you tell me more about Ward and you?" Jade handed her a shoulder bag and carried one for herself. They weren't empty, and when she looked inside hers, there were bundles of blankets. Outside, the white mountain glared from the sun; even without a rising, burning feeling, Rosalina had to force her eyes to stay open as they adjusted.

"Well, he's like a brother to me. I'll need to stay here for a while and prepare some new animals for wherever I'll be moving. If I didn't have him to fall back to, I wouldn't have a way to move forward. Every time I have lost a home or needed to leave some-where suddenly, he has been my rock." It becomes obvious shortly after they start walking that they are tracking rabbits. With the hard crunch of snow underfoot, most critters scattered long before they came close. "it would be easier to catch them at night" Jade says practically reading her mind. "But It's a tradition Ward lets me enjoy the sun with his jewelry. I get to try things as humanly as possible. Normally, it's just me, so if we can't get anything, at least I've spent the time with you."

The sentiment would have made Rosalina blush, but instead, she mumbled an equally affectionate 'smooth talker,' earning a wink from Jade. Even on a vacant mountain in the daylight, they can't just go sprinting around, making what could have been a 20-minute task turn into a few hours one bunny for each of them. Jade explained why she'd accept one but not another generally to do with their age; not too young to need their mom's formula but not too old, it would be harder to make them adjust to the purpose they were meant for.

Snow crunched under the weight of their strides, the weight in their bags squirmed, and no more animals could be found after trek-king as far out as the tiny bunnies could bear to be; so, for all these reasons, they started back, careful not to jostle them. Feeling bad that her presence must have made retrieving the desired four animals that Jade had once before impossible. Despite the silence between them during their search, it wasn't strange, nor did Jade seem to be bothered as they returned with only two bunnies. Rosalina, for her part, was silent as she puzzled over how Jade would be here while she was home in Hell's Kitchen until she couldn't help but let a question slip.

"Your job wouldn't understand the loss of equipment and the new sudden move again?" Skipping all the questions like who would visit who? How often? Or was she done training? Rosalina took Jade by surprise, asking this. Making it back inside and securing the door before Jade took the bunnies out, having a good look at them, she didn't put off answering her as if suspecting it would come up, just not so right on the head.

"I probably could make something believable up, but if I did and they wanted police records or insurance claims filed, I just wouldn't have the means to deal with all that attention. Ward is as cautious as he is for the same reason: we don't have the honest documents to provide, so we move on and start over." Saying this, as they went down into the cellar, the warmth in the house faded slightly, making the words weigh on Rosalina, but Jade prepared two separate cages with shredded lettuce and hay. Once latched and looking as comfortable as no newly homed wild animals could, they left them to find peace with the situation. Rosalina had given her thanks for the lengths Jade had taken to save her, but only then could Rosalina find the words that she'd been unable to say before.

"I know I don't know everything I'm in for now, and despite what has been the wildest few weeks, I hope you could never regret saving me." At this, Jade looks shocked she would even have to ask. "I just mean, look at all the trouble it caused you. Even if you had avoided it for so long and would have had to face it all eventually, at least it would have been on your terms and not as much damage to your life."

After a moment, looking stunned, Jade becomes torn as she looks down at the ground and then back up as Rosalina watches her wring her hands. For what seemed like minutes, Jade waited; it wasn't until they walked through the small kitchen living room to the fireplace that Jade, who was only a few steps ahead of Rosalina, suddenly spun on her heels. Now they stood face to face, the look in her eyes trying to express what she now looked ready to say. Believing there is a look of nervousness in her expression, Rosalina swallows, finding it not helpful. Instead, she took Jade's hand reassuringly and squeezed; even if she felt her words had gotten away from her, Jade should be allowed to say anything she needed.

"I have to admit I could have stepped in sooner and stopped you from being hurt at all, but for so many reasons, I told myself it wasn't necessary. I would get caught, or you would find out what I was, and on and on. When I did, I felt almost relieved. You changed, and I felt something I would never have thought I could. I spent so long running, and even with your great-grandparents learning what I was, I never thought I could be truly connected to someone. Ward and the group do make sure I feel I have a family. They are all like brothers, sisters, and mothers; I won't lose them from a natural death since they are immortal. You are different, and I feel so horrible saying it this way, but I have a companion in you. It doesn't have to be forever, but like the group, you aren't mortal. I feel so much freer to be me and damned be the rest. I don't care where I am or if I start over again and again so long as I can share anything with you. Even the truth that I failed you, which I would totally understand if you needed your space from me..."

Rosalina's lips parted to say something, then closed. It felt like she was handing her heart over at her confession of feelings only to have Jade thrust hers right at her in return. It had felt like something was there all along, unsaid and heavy; now it was present, and every other guilty or consuming thought felt lighter than ever. Nothing could make her desire a different life now that she'd experienced far more than she'd ever imagined, nor could Rosalina find the anger Jade expected of her simply because she knew that the past was the past. Nothing could cure her, but fortunately, she didn't want that, not really.

Jade's confession sounded more like an attempted admission of deep feelings. Love didn't stop Rosalina from returning to her life as a baker entrepreneur, and it wouldn't. Suddenly, her lips are trembling nervously; she stills them with a swipe of her tongue over them. Clasping Jade's hands tighter in hers so her reaction isn't taken the wrong way to cause Jade to pull away. Rosalina leans forward, washing away the doubts and worries buried in their confessions between them with a delicate kiss.

"I love you too." She said with a whisper but without hesitation and found she could say it again and again, so she did. "I love you. Your decision to save me when you did and my fears of ruining what you built in Hell's Kitchen are proof of more between us. I suppose we will have to learn to stop worrying and enjoy this feeling a little bit."

"Yes, I think I'd like to focus on that." Jade had heard and said claims of love before, but as the term of endearment left Rosalina's mouth, they were left forgotten in her past as her own and Rosalina's emotions mingled among the bond between them. In a synced motion, they stepped to each other, their lips pressed against each other again. Jade ran her hand the length of Rosalina's arm, burying her fingers at the base of her head where the hair had slightly grown in. Heat crested close to them as if the flame was trying to reach out, and as it did, it melted the moment into a memory. Melding together

Rosalina's honeysuckle and cedar fragrance with citrus from the red cedar wood in the fire.

Rosalina lays her hand over Jade's collarbone before trailing her smooth, pointed fingernails along Jade's skin until the edge of her jawline is pressed underneath Rosalina's palm, and her fingers lace around the base of her ear. Minutes pass under each other's touch as an array of sensations sparked them into a passionate kiss. Time could have gone forever without notice if not for the faint snaps beside them. When they separate next, Jade catches her bottom lip between her teeth, observing the delicate dance of shadows not just around the room but also over Rosalina; the effects of the sun, as it thinned or stretched what ones flickered across Rosalina's Pale skin, did not escape Jade making her almost speechless.

"Now, that is something I will never forget," Rosalina whispers, looking just as dazed as Jade, in a way that tells her that what she, too, experienced was more than an ordinary romantic kiss for eternal beings. Sharing a faint chuckle, Jade sweeps Rosalina's bangs from her face. The touch across her cheeks felt different, stirring a shiver down Rosalina's spine. Noticing the reaction, Jade leaned in to give her a soft, lingering kiss.

Arching into the embrace, Rosalina brought her hands over Jade's hips. Electricity fired between them as Jade's lips found Rosalina's neck, her fangs grazing over the skin. In response, Rosalina gripped the fabric of Jade's jeans under her fingers as a soft moan escaped her lips. Closing her eyelids, the room around them disappeared.

Effortlessly, like a dance, Jade led Rosalina a few steps back. Her back pressed against the mantel, the solid support catching her as she melted under the sweet and seductive embrace when their lips met again in a fiery kiss. Nothing needed to be said as the pace slowed, and Jade lightly brushed her forehead against hers, clearing the passion calmly. Rosalina understood the desire to deepen their connection, which conflicted with the yearning to know one another better they both shared.

Jade gazed at her apologetically while easing herself off of Rosalina. Like the gentlewoman she was, Jade scooped up her hand and took a step back, bringing Rosalina from the mantle. Having lost their senses momentarily, they found themselves at a crossroads. A tender expression reveals their mutual understanding as they lock their gaze.

A dream-like sigh from Phantom brings them back to the truth of where they were. Embarrassment flashed through Rosalina, but it was quickly washed away with a light touch from Jade's hand on her shoulder. A reminder that she was not alone in having forgotten the place was not theirs, even if the silence of the cabin was misleading. Snow thuds from the window to the deck outside as Jade opens her mouth, bringing sunshine to the room and lightening the tension as she speaks.

"Rose...I have been waiting forever to be so open with someone. With you, that's finally what I feel I can do. Admitting that I feel the beginnings of love makes me a little eager to know more about you. I have so much I feel more able to ask or to share without Gabriel around." Rosalina's eyes sparkle at the shortened name, giving Jade enough confidence to follow through to the end of what she said. Softly, Jade pecks Rosalina's lips once more, cupping Rosalina's hands as she starts stronger this time. "With senses like ours, we could get carried away, as you can tell. I was actually hoping we could get to know each other better."

"Of course, that sounds wonderful." With the passionate interest eased to the sideline, they made their way over to the table, Rosalina beaming at the opportunity, showing more of her excitement than she'd like, yet with a moment like what they just shared, she couldn't help if she sounded and looked brighter. "You go first ask anything. We can trade off."

Jade thought for a few moments; since she had gotten closer to the woman she had saved, she'd been protective of exposing information about her life, knowing Gabriel could learn of something to hurt her or even both of them. Obviously, he hadn't discovered or didn't care about her relationships with her chosen family; if he had, she expected he would have approached the situation sooner. Her reluctance to share was gone now that he could no longer hold any of her past over her. There was a great many things Jade had never shared before; now, she wanted to share them with Rosalina and even learn the depth of Rosalina's humanity and the life she carries.

"Tell me about your family. Even though they don't approve of all of you, did you have someone you told first?" It came out of nowhere, but when the thought of what to ask crossed her mind, Jade wanted to know who Rosalina looked up to or didn't. Rosalina heard the question and pinched her eyes closed, leading Jade to expect a rush of emotions. Rosalina appeared to be trying to tame them. Successfully, she laid her hands flat on the table, using it to ground herself at the question. Jade resisted the urge to take the question back because she hoped Rosalina would answer.

"Gosh, well, I guess the first time I told anyone, it was this girl in school. I thought she was so beautiful I had to ask her to go to a dance. It went pretty smoothly, so I told my aunt. She was so supportive and said she hoped I would feel like telling the family one day. Her kindness made what happened with my parents seem unusual and unnecessary. Their disapproval went on for years, dismissing my interests, refusing to meet my girlfriends, and fighting about who I'd marry one day. It wasn't until after my father passed that my mother stopped holding back, I guess. Demanded I never reveal my interests to the rest of the family. One day, one of my cousins was talking about kids, and I said I'd have to consider adopting. Which sounded confusing so I just blurted out how expensive two women having a baby would be." Rosalina strained herself as she said this and gave an embarrassed grin as she finished.

"I spent so long around men and a woman that was obsessed with a man that I had no idea until some time after I went on my own. I was around two hundred years old before the realization came to me. A market vendor who made silk, she often walked home late. We flirted sometimes, but when I admitted my feelings, she exclaimed she had a husband and wouldn't separate her family. I didn't have a family to tell until much later. I was discreet about my interest until the last 50 years." Jade said, sharing her story after hearing Rosalina's so they could feel equally exposed. When Rosalina asked her question, it was easily becoming a pattern.

They'd shared about any significant partners and whether either had been with a man. While Jade had never been with a guy, Rosalina once dated a guy or two to sate her family's interest in her dating life in high school. Eventually, she came to a point when she realized how important it was to be true to herself, leading her to come out to her entire family. In the transition to other topics, Rosalina asked if Jade had found a way to attend college, if she had any siblings, and what her favorite cover job had been. Jade had been more curious to know if Rosalina enjoyed her trip to Paris in high school, if she liked sailing or preferred large ships, and what her favorite things to do for fun were.

10 ▎

Family Matters

Over the next few hours, Rosalina and Jade chatted, sometimes ending up on sore topics and other times, they would share and begin laughing. It was a surprise Ward hadn't woken sooner, but it was turning quickly into evening when he came out in a cozy robe. Drifting straight to the small counter in the kitchen, reached for a teacup, looked at it, then decided against it, put it back, and dragged out a coffee mug. Almost instantly, Rosalina believes she should offer to use her skills but thinks better of it considering his age, so instead, she offers to take Phantom out for the first time since the airport.

To everyone's surprise, the softer-than-expected scurry of scrapping sounds against the flooring brought attention to his form, having gone back down to a puppy again. The events that encouraged his transformation were over, leaving him with a smaller stride. Not discouraged, though, he looked eager to head outside. With his size and the lack of a leash by the door, Rosalina slipped out with Phantom, not expecting him to be able to run very far on her.

The sun faced them as it went down; the white hill of the mountain loomed over the distant cities of New York, which began flickering lights on as the evening crept closer. The wind picked up, spreading a thin curtain of snow over the view before settling again. Phantom, though tiny, trotted through the thick layers, leaving the slightest of trials wherever he went. She followed him distantly in case he had any trouble in his current size.

Off in the distance, high above them, still was even more mountain, some covered in trees; a howl echoed, followed by a chorus of howls from the whole pack. The start of a growl came from Phantom but quickly turned into a howl. Unfortunately, it was so faint in comparison to what they just heard. Realizing this, Phantom whined and took to lying where he was surrounded by snow in a display of how sad he felt in his loneliness. Though he had Ward and even her now, he still desired to return to his pack, and from the sounds of it, they already had a new leader.

"Hey," she said to him, waiting for him to pick up his head at least. When he did, she walked the short way to the porch and sat there; he just stared after her. "oh, come here, will you." She wasn't cold, but she knew he must be starting to feel a bit chilly. Trotting over to her, he kept his head down and curled sadly at the foot of the porch, giving a little huff as he did. "I know you want to go back home. I promise I will help. I'll even ask Ward if he knows someone who can help. For now, you have to stay; you'll be safer. You know that otherwise, you could have left long before now. I promise to get you back to your family."

They sat there on the steps for a few minutes, Rosalina sitting criss-cross knees angled downward, petting his thick snow-covered fur, until he reached his head up and put it on her lap. Traces of crystal tears brimmed his eyes; aware of his true nature, his brown-yellowish eyes looked older and more hurt than his age appeared to be. Thumbing the bridge of his nose a few times before she pats the space on the step beside her and lifts her knees so Phantom would follow her back inside. Although he still looked disheartened, he followed her only to curl up by the fire.

"What happened?" Ward asked, looking at Phantom worriedly, perhaps having heard the commotion outside.

"He heard his pack howling and tried to return it. He couldn't be heard, not at the size he is." Rosalina answered, keeping her voice low, not intending to sound less sensitive to Phantom's cursed state as she answered. Pulling back a chair to sit at the table again, Rosalina looked back at where Phantom lay, feeling the weight of what she promised Phantom. "So, Ward, what do you think we can do to help him?"

Joining them, Ward sips his coffee with a fixed curl of distaste on his lips. Picking up the lid off a sugar cube holder, he puts two cubes in, stirs it gently, and sips once more, all while tapping the rim of his cup in thought. Ward stands up a few sips later, running his hands over his robe, magically turning them into what appeared to be his usual suit, only this time it was purple. Walking over to Phantom, Ward runs his fingers through his coat and whispers to him before taking some of his loose fur and some plucked fur separately.

"I learned some things from Sage, tests and spells. That's about all I can do with the magic she does. In this case, I would rather have Sage run the tests herself. Perhaps this will be of use to her if I have assumed right. I'll ask her to meet up soon." He places them into bags.

"Sage tried teaching you. Why when you already have magic?" Rosalina asks, mostly curious about what their differences are.

"I can't truly use any of it. Testing for poison, traces of magic, and such I can do, but it has its limits to how direct the information is. For example, I might know there is poison but not what kind; I can sense magic but not follow its trail. Another difference is I don't rely on the energy I consume. I get tired, just like anyone else, after focusing on so much at once. Still, magic is natural to me, not the same as drawing energy in and reusing it." As he finished explaining, though not precisely how his power worked, Rosalina caught the tail end of her ringtone coming from an end table where hers and Jade's things were sitting. Not expecting anyone to be contacting her, she tried to grab it in time, but it was buried in the backpack they'd brought.

"I hope it's not my job or something. Where? Oh, never mind, I got it." Finding her phone, a voicemail pops up with a ding. It hadn't been able to be useful overseas, so she left it behind; beyond that, she thought there was no cell reception on the mountain anyway. It had picked up a few other messages, none from her job, but the most recent was from her cousin. "Strange... it's my cousin."

Rosalina's eyebrows knitted as she looked at the notification of two missed calls, one yesterday after they all left to go to her apartment and one now. Her finger hovered over the screen, worried and hesitant to face anyone in her family as she was now. However, she decided it couldn't hurt to listen to the voicemail he left.

"I take it that's unusual?" Jade asks, a hint of concern showing. Rosalina could feel her hopes to protect Rosalina from anything willing to hurt her. Looking at her, Rosalina gives her an appreciative smile before answering, still putting the phone to her ear.

"He hasn't spoken to me as much this last couple of years and definitely hasn't called me before." Once she heard his shaken and slightly angered voice fretting about one thing or another, all of which she could barely make sense of, she wanted to urgently call him back, which he picked up at once. Ward couldn't hear, but to Jade, it was impossible not to listen to both sides of the call.

"Hey Rosie, I know it's been a while. Thanks for calling me back." He sounded better but stuffy. "I know it's not fair to ask out of nowhere, but I need somewhere to stay for a few days. I can't explain over the phone. I just left home...please, I will figure something else out in a few days. I just-"

"Darius, it's okay. Really, it's okay. I'm not home right now, but I could be home if you give me a couple of hours." As she spoke, she mentally listed everything that needed to be prepared. Her fridge needed to be cleaned, fresh food needed to be bought, and so on.

"Deal, I'm not going to make it to Hell's Kitchen before a few hours anyways. Thank you, cuz." Relief filled his voice, even if she could still hear him sniff every so often.

"of course! I'll send you my address in a text. See you soon." She hung up, speedily texted her address, then turned to face the other pair. Lifting her hands in surrender, she exclaimed she had to head out now. Unlike the worry she felt about returning to the city before Gabriel ruined everything, she felt confident that she could control herself for her cousin's sake. She'd expected a debate or something from Jade, but even she seemed to understand how important it was to her.

"Well, before you go, you'll need to feed if you don't have time I can give you a bag. If you like, I'll stop in and bring you a secret supply and something to conceal them in your fridge." Ward kindly offers given the news. Jade grimaced slightly at the suggestion of consuming human blood but said nothing about that.

"Ready to travel on your own or-" Now it was Jade's phone that rang, cutting her off. Ward remarked on how much he disliked phones sometimes but gestured for her to decide quickly, leaving it up to her to enter the kitchen towards the cellar or not; she nodded but let him lead the way. Answering the call, Jade stretched her neck stiff as she heard a rasped voice over the line. She left the room without a word to give Jade some privacy. Whoever was on the line sounded weakened by sobs not afflicting them now, not that Ward would have caught it, but Rosalina had.

"I only offer this so freely with you being new and all because you seem to have a bit more control than Jade did. I won't share her story, but I like to think of the difference as if it is just like drugs. Some people have a drug, and they are perfectly fine; others, they spiral either a bad effect or an addiction occurs." In his cellar were colored lights of blue and purple leading them down the stairs. He pulled a fresh bag from the mini teal fridge.

"You might want to check on that call. It sounded important." Rosalina says, taking the cold bag from him, unsure if he would want to know.

"Take your time. I'll see if it was someone from the group, at least. Not sure Jade would give anyone else her number, but still." He hurried up the steps, leaving Rosalina alone. Jade's tense expression replays in her mind, making it harder to pace herself. Tearing open the corner like Jade had before, she squeezed the metallic liquid from the bag and finished it quickly. Tossing the bag, she checked her face with a wipe of her hand and used the sink in the kitchen to wash her hands as she came up from the cellar.

"H-Hey, I'll be there as soon as possible, I promise. I'm with Ward right now. Don't let yourself get caught there, even if whoever did this is long gone, but don't let anyone disturb anything. I'll come look, but we should get a hold of Lyra, too. She's much more capable at reaching everyone to bring them together, and so we can figure out who would do something so awful." Ward supported Jade's weight as she leaned her hand and gradually her body against his shoulder. "Let me tell Ward, and we'll be there in no time. Bye"

Hanging up the phone, a cry escaped Jade, prompting Rosalina to rush to her side. Ward wrapped Jade into his arms, not bothering to ask anything just yet. Only a few minutes pass before Jade presses her hands, which had been balled up, flatly onto his suit as she twists free and tries to smooth the wrinkles made by her. Wiping her eyes, she choked out a summary of what had been said to her in just a few words.

"Dylan was killed." Rosalina was never one to gasp usually, but she did now, never having known anyone who lost someone who was killed. Sick, accidental, or elderly death but never an intentional death. Still looking at Ward, Jade says. "We have to go. It was displayed she thinks it was a message of some kind."

"Yeah, we have to." Ward agrees, his hand over his mouth, muffling his response, but then drops into a seat. Jade followed, grasping his hand tightly.

"I can... stay here or go with you instead of-"Rosalina tried to offer, kneeling between them, not only voicing her concern but showing it by putting a comforting hand out to their joined hands.

"No, Rose, it's sweet of you, but this sounds serious, even potentially dangerous. We'll go help her for a few days, then we can come back for you once we've made some arrangements."

"Phantom," Ward calls out with silent tears streaming down his face. Immediately, tiny pitter patters of Phantom's nails come up to them; his tail wags excitedly at first, then phantom tilts his head before deciding to work his way between them all. Touching his nose to Ward's free hand and nudging it upward, Phantom finally got Ward to set his hand on the top of his head, to pet him. Ward sniffled, bringing his other hand from Jade and Rosalina's grasp to ruffle Phantom's soft fur a little more. "We are gonna go somewhere a little warmer, but I think you'll like it."

One at a time, they break apart from the small huddle. Jade looked as if she didn't move; the weight of her emotions could keep her in place forever. Her eyes were dark with a sadness that Rosalina couldn't imagine. If Dylan were part of her group even half the time since Jade met Ward, it would still be hard to lose someone you've known for decades, though it sounded more like centuries.

"The council," Jade said, breaking the silence. Ward nods, grabbing a pen and paper, understanding what she means.

"I will ask if it's likely to be related to their agent." Scribbling through his letter quickly and taking no time to envelope it before making it disappear in a puff of smoke. "Hopefully, Thalia is in."

Rosalina looked over the cabin, knowing her time limit was already creeping close, but leaving felt surreal. The short time that had passed since her change remade the part of Rosalina that once desired to be alone. The mental image of returning to the city alone and surrounded by blood oddly felt less complicated and desirable now than a separate image of whatever dangerous path Jade had to face. The promise of only a few days was all Rosalina could hold onto as she said her goodbyes, steeling her courage as she took off down the hillside of the mountain.

Concurrently, Ward brought Phantom and Jade to Dylan's home in Illinois, landing them in the middle of the field to the left of the manor. Jade strikes off on her toes towards the front door, looking for signs of damage. Not finding any, she spun toward the barn where the only other person waiting for them would be. With her phone still in hand, Adreana clings to the barn doorway for support until Ward wraps her up in his arms, letting Jade enter the barn to inspect it without worrying about leaving her alone.

A few times when lying awake, Jade would feel the returning sensations of growing waves, salt in the air, and the creaking of wet wood. This time, however, it wasn't how she recalled those times at sea and the wrongs she'd done. The sight of a dried pool of blood dragged back each and every loss of control that led to a gruesome scene much like the one before her. It was a display that Jade couldn't pull her eyes from, no matter how much pain it caused to see pieces of her friend chained to the ceiling of his own barn.

Dylan lived a calm life in the middle of nowhere, so whoever did this was not still here because they had to have no idea when the body would be found. Illinois is not full of equestrian estates or farms, southern Illinois of the few exceptions; Jade struggled to hold back the sadness threatening to release, remembering all the times she could find peace when visiting Dylan. There was even the Shawnee forest to hunt when she needed to feed. Whoever or whatever brought this loss to the group and Adreana, his partner, would pay.

Adreana's muffled sobs into Ward's neck begged for Jade to see everything, perhaps something they could not. Dylan's blood was left to drain after being used to inscribe a message. Of course, Jade had never been so cruel, but death was monstrous enough. Seeing this and the message, 'the hunt begins,' stirs a furious rage that she quickly releases, remembering her new prodigy's connection to emotions. Hoping Rosalina didn't feel it, Jade reflects on her crimes, asking herself if it was a hunt she deserved or something else entirely.

Her first bloody death, Gabriel cleaned up and only reprimanded her for the indecency of making a mess. Jade knew she had cleaned up her mess after months of starving on a ship filled with British colonists headed to America. She'd joined the ships disguised as Jacob back then, only failing to understand how long the trip would take. Her persistence to not feed on the humans and animals aboard forced her into a deep sleep-like hibernation.

After being mistaken for dead and thrown from the ship, she awoke forced to swim out of sight to shore and regretfully killed many animals to satisfy her hunger, all of which she didn't leave showing off her deadly skills or taunting a message. The ship and its passengers were lucky by all accounts, for many years later, Jade encountered a similar problem and regretfully killed a whole crew that she'd come to be close with. All because the trips to land she'd requested were without their rewards. Of course, anyone who found the ship didn't know the reasons it had been left to be considered lost at sea, covered in blood, and filled with losses.

None of these experiences gave Jade the understanding that the situation needed. Doing her best, she faces Ward and Adreana. The petite woman neither has the power to reach the body nor the physical abilities to do it alone. It is clear they will need to work together.

"Lyra will want to know," Jade whispers, the beginnings of the ideas forming in her mind. "Obviously, it's a message, but for supernaturals in general or specifically someone who knew Dylan?"

"I don't know," Adreana says, sniffing her nose into her hand and then briefly gravitating herself from Ward to hug Jade in relief that she had come too. "He didn't deserve this; I just know it."

"Of course not," Ward says, finally able to regain his voice. After supporting Adreana as he had, he still needed to comfort himself and gestured for Phantom to come. The little puppy form takes his saddened eyes off the corpse and lifts his head from his paws to stand and walk to him. Immediately, Ward picks him up, and Phantom uncharacteristically licks his hands.

After calling their leader and getting Dylan from the barn's roof, they prepared a temporary means to keep his body and materials used to clean up. An ice-cold fear struck Jade when only the latter was left to do. It was only clear the sensation was through her bond with Rosalina when the fear intensified and morphed into a protective rage. Dropping her brushes and rags, she yells for Ward.

"Ward! Someone is...Rosalina is in danger." He flicks his eyes up momentarily at the horrific sight that remains and throws his equipment down, too.

"For your protection, I have to send you two to my cabin." Concern for them spreads over Adreana's face as things unravel. "We will be right back, I swear." He says equally to Phantom and Adreana, grasping Jade's hand and simultaneously disappearing and transporting Phantom and Adreana with no more time to explain. One destination seemed possible with how long they'd been and knowing Rosalina should have been home by now. With her cousin there or not, it seemed the only choice under such circumstances.

Meanwhile, once or twice on the descent, Rosalina's thoughts left the white expanse before her and began wandering ahead to what could have caused Darius to need her at such a specific time. Focusing on his troubles and potential needs kept her from anticipating the grief Jade would surely feel when they made it to where they were headed. When it came, it was clear she could never have prepared for it as Rosalina's vision blurred. Instinctively, she avoided trees in the way, but as a deep wave of loss and anger came, Rosalina pushed off so hard she launched from the side of the mountain.

As the wind seemed to let her fly, spots of red bled into sight. Unsure if she saw spots of red as some trick of the light or if it was pieces of what Jade was seeing coming through, Rosalina landed with a tumble. Rolling and kicking up snow until she could twist her legs out ahead to self-assert herself. Rosalina dug her feet into the snow as deep as she could until the friction brought her to a complete stop.

In the time that fixing her clothes and shaking out the snow buried in them took, the feelings were gone. She looked up to where the misstep happened, miles and miles between, and then down to see how much further she had. Rosalina carefully started again, putting more focus on Darius, remembering when they were younger; his parents split, how his mother sent him to schools known to allow only Black kids, and despite his father's wishes, even a historically

Black college. They were thick as thieves growing up until school took over their lives; Rosalina remembered her uncle wanted him to have more connection to people than just the color of his skin, ultimately causing Darius's parents to separate.

None of this troubled Darius, though Rosalina saw plenty of mixed kids take it hard. Something serious must have happened if he could handle all that without cracking. All she could think about was what she could do to help. Her great-grandmother, whom Jade had saved, had been mixed; the color of other people's skin, especially with how fair most of her family happened to be, was not as much of a struggle in her family as it was to Darius's mother. She resolved her thoughts, knowing that whatever happened must have been one big mess as she finally found herself in familiar cities.

Once back in Hell's Kitchen, after pushing herself as fast as she could while still being cautious and as attentive as Jade showed her, Rosalina slipped out of a darkened side street beside the still-open grocery store a few blocks from her apartment. Her mind still split on the two situations holding her attention, she absentmindedly grabbed a basket filling it with food she'd known Darius to like in the past. The mental distractions keep her from thinking even for a moment about the number of people around her. Only when coming up to her apartment to see Darius thumping his foot nervously as he sat on the bottom steps waiting for her, did she feel her attention fully drawn into the situation before her.

A wild thought crossed Rosalina's mind a block away, with him still not seeing her. Jade never said mortals couldn't be told. He might be able to keep her secret, but a part of her expected that even if he kept it, Darius might never speak to her again. That alone kept any further ideas at bay as he spots her and jumps to his feet, covering up his worries with a wide grin to greet her, which Rosalina mirrors.

"Dari!" Rosalina exclaims, putting the bags in her hands down and wrapping him in a hug. She squeezes him, taking in his health momentarily before pulling back, burning with questions. "Is Uncle Pete okay? Your mom?"

"Yeah, Rosie, they are fine. I'm sorry to worry you; it's nothing like that." He brushes back his grown-out hair, running his fingers the length of the thick coiled curls. "When I say it, I know it will make it worse that I never reached out sooner. I'm not ashamed, honest. I've just never liked adding more stress to my life, and well, I had a fight with my mom...it just came out."

"Hey, take a deep breath. We can go up, and you can tell me everything." She watched him as he shook his head, noticing a long earring swaying as he did so. So much had changed, she thought as she took in each one.

"No, I have to say this first, then you can decide. I'm gay, Rosie, and I feel horrible that I'm coming to you in the same way you left expecting you to help me." Darius says, on the verge of tears.

"So. I mean, wow, thank you for saying that, but we're family. I'm just glad I can offer you someplace to figure things out. Anyway, let's go up. I wasn't home, so I figured I'd get some fresh food in case anything went bad while I was gone." He looks relieved as she ushers him up to the main entrance while she grabs the bags again. Rummaging for her keys, she tosses them to him, telling him the apartment number, and they head inside the main doors. Guilt swelled at her harmless lie, knowing he wouldn't understand if her truth was as easy to say as he was.

They entered the building, Rosalina not even sparing a glance upward as she did. She might have seen the flicker of a shadow across the curtains of the room facing the street. She might not have kept chatting as they climbed a set of stairs. Nor would she have let

Darius open her door and enter, where he returned her question of if he was still in school or not with a scream.

...to be continued!

About The Author

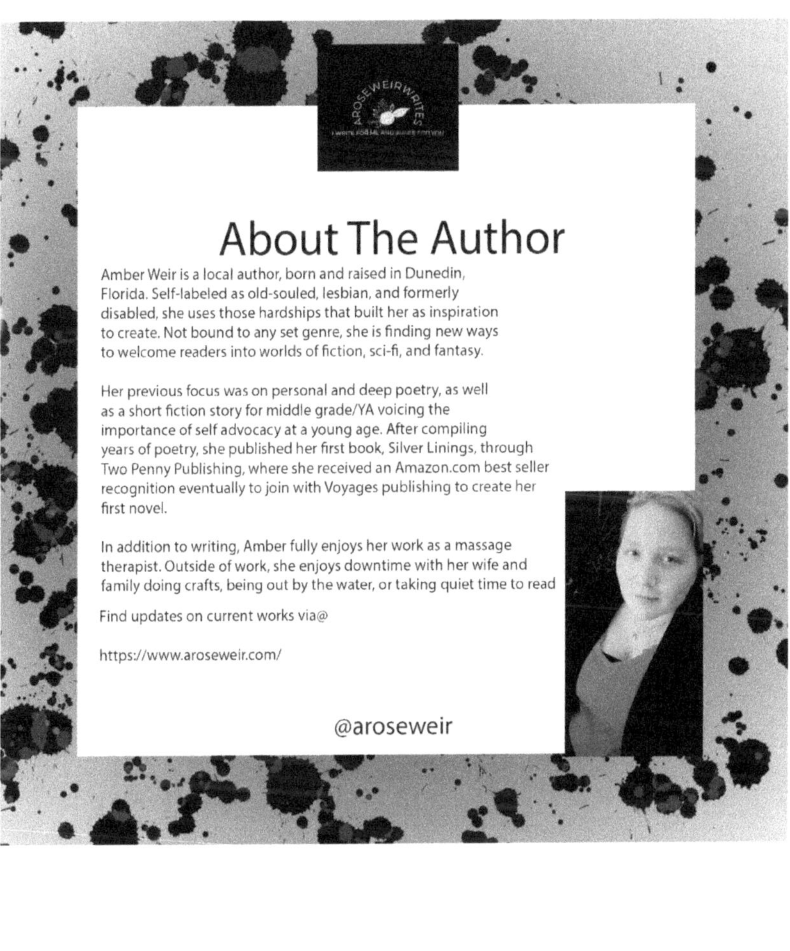

Amber Weir is a local author, born and raised in Dunedin, Florida. Self-labeled as old-souled, lesbian, and formerly disabled, she uses those hardships that built her as inspiration to create. Not bound to any set genre, she is finding new ways to welcome readers into worlds of fiction, sci-fi, and fantasy.

Her previous focus was on personal and deep poetry, as well as a short fiction story for middle grade/YA voicing the importance of self advocacy at a young age. After compiling years of poetry, she published her first book, Silver Linings, through Two Penny Publishing, where she received an Amazon.com best seller recognition eventually to join with Voyages publishing to create her first novel.

In addition to writing, Amber fully enjoys her work as a massage therapist. Outside of work, she enjoys downtime with her wife and family doing crafts, being out by the water, or taking quiet time to read

Find updates on current works via@

https://www.aroseweir.com/

@aroseweir